SUSAN
AND
HER
CLASSIC
CONVERTIBLE

SUSAN
AND
HER
CLASSIC
CONVERTIBLE

W. E. Butterworth

Four Winds Press / New York

Second Printing, 1971

Published by Four Winds Press
A Division of Scholastic Magazines, Inc., New York, N.Y.

Copyright © 1970 by W. E. Butterworth

SUSAN
AND
HER
CLASSIC
CONVERTIBLE

I

More than once it had occurred to Susan Hebard, who was seventeen, that she might have been better off if she'd been a boy. She believed that it *was* a man's world, and she really didn't have much faith in the Civil Rights Act of 1964, at least insofar as it promised equal rights to women.

There was a case in point before her. She had a summer job as a lifeguard at the Fairfield Country Club, which sounded a good deal more elegant than it really was. She had applied to an advertisement which announced that "applications were being accepted for lifeguard jobs," and listing the qualifications: over sixteen, and possessing the American Red Cross Senior Life Saving Certificate.

She had just turned seventeen, and she had had no trouble whatever in getting through the Red Cross examination. But when she went to Mr. Haggerty, who was in charge of the pool and the tennis courts, and announced she wanted a job, she got what she had grown to call the standard, "Well, I don't know," reply.

"You were thinking of boys, right?" she had challenged.

"As a matter of fact, Susan, yes," Mr. Haggerty had replied, his tone of voice indicating that he was relieved she understood.

"Why?" she had asked, and that had sort of thrown him off balance.

"If someone were in trouble in the water, how could you get them out?"

"The same way I dragged Randy out when I took the test," she replied. Randy was her cousin Randolph Hebard Ward, aged nineteen, who had been more or less the bane of her existence as long as she could remember. Randy, though, had not been very cooperative as a simulated drowning victim when she'd tried to pull him out of the pool.

But she had pulled him out, and Mr. Haggerty had been there watching, so that question was resolved in her favor.

"You're the only girl who has applied," Mr. Haggerty said.

"I'm the only girl around here with the Senior Certificate," she'd answered.

He backed up again. "I'll let you know, Susan," he said.

The issue had been resolved by giving all fifteen applicants (fourteen boys and Susan) a test for the six jobs open. The test had included both speed and endurance swimming

8

tests, as well as a rerun of the "save the drowning man" portion of the Red Cross examination.

She'd placed third in the speed test, had had no trouble at all making ten laps of the pool, and her drowning victim had been a pretty nice guy, who hadn't overplayed his resistance when she hauled him to safety.

In other words, she'd won fair and square. Mr. Haggerty had given her the job.

But she quickly found out that she was not going to be permitted to reign like some latter-day Greek god from the pinnacle of the lifeguard platform. This, as a result of a gentleman's agreement, was to be the masculine prerogative of the boys. They had something else in mind for Susan.

At the club there were a large number of children who could not swim, and whose parents thought that someone else could teach them better than they could. And everyone agreed that Susan Hebard, who swam so well, was so understanding, and, after all, was a girl, would be the ideal lifeguard to teach them.

Mr. Haggerty was more or less fair about it. He admitted that teaching kids to swim was a bit harder than just sitting around waiting for someone to call for help, or majestically blowing a whistle at various sinners guilty of breaking pool regulations, and he told her that he would give her credit for double time while she taught.

In other words, if she taught two two-hour swimming classes every day, she would be given credit for eight hours of work. She fought down the terrible temptation to shove

Mr. Haggerty in the pool to see if *he* could swim and accepted the proposition. There were a number of reasons for her decision, the most important one being that she suspected that Mr. Haggerty hoped she would turn it down.

With several notable exceptions, her students were good kids, and she soon enjoyed teaching most of them. Two of the exceptions were girls, one fat and one thin, both aged nine, and both of whom Susan believed should be kept in a cage. The third was a seven-year-old boy who liked water only when it was in a glass with ice cubes, and held the firm belief that Susan was cheerfully trying to drown him.

The others wanted to learn, and it wasn't long before Susan had proudly sent a half dozen of them over to Mr. Haggerty for the "Beyond the Ropes" test, which consisted of a full length swim of the pool. After passing this test they were allowed to go beyond the shallow-end ropes and jump off the diving boards.

All in all, as the summer passed, Susan was glad that she'd had the guts to stay on. For one thing, it occurred to her that she would really have been bored to tears just sitting on the platform under the umbrella. For another, she was actually making twice as much money as the boys; or, at least, working only half the time for the same money, which was even better. She had time to play tennis, and, when her father could get away from the clinic and the hospital, to play nine holes of golf with him.

It was, she realized, a much better way to pass the summer, even without considering her pay, than the way the other girls were spending it. They were generally clustered around the lifeguard platforms, giggling.

It wasn't that Susan didn't like the male gender. It was just that she couldn't see demonstrating her interest in them by hanging on their every word, since some of the words they uttered were hardly immortal, philosophical, or even particularly interesting.

Susan's idea of the male role in the scheme of things had gotten her in trouble before. She was the only girl in her "crowd" at either the country club or Fairfield High who did not have a "very best" girl friend, and she felt that this was a direct result of her unwillingness to devote every waking moment to the attraction of the male animal.

When she saw her father's car, the battered old Buick that he used for housecalls and for running back and forth between the hospital and the clinic, she looked at her watch.

It was half-past two; her lesson ran for another half an hour. She supposed that for once the waiting room hadn't been full at closing time, and her father had taken off early. Well, that was better than what usually happened when they had a golf date: a telephone call from either the hospital or the clinic, with Miss Hoag's or a nurse's voice telling her that there was an emergency, or a waiting room full of people, or a baby about to arrive, and that her father said to tell her he was sorry he couldn't make it.

Her afternoon class was the wee-ones, the four-, five-, and six-year-olds, some of them just now progressing to the point where they had learned how to breathe in the pool.

She couldn't take her eyes off them long enough to watch where her father went with the car.

Susan was surprised when Mr. Haggerty suddenly appeared in the pool beside her.

"I'll take over for the rest of the hour," he said. "Your father's waiting for you over there."

She looked at the pool gate, and saw her father walking away, back to the Buick. She climbed out of the pool, found a towel, and dried herself as she walked down along the edge of the pool and out of the fenced-in area after him.

When she got to the car he leaned over and opened the door for her. Then he put his medical bag on the seat. She sensed immediately that something was very wrong.

"What's the matter?" she asked.

Her father looked at her. "I've always believed the best way to deliver bad news is to deliver it without beating around the bush. Susan, I just had a call from the General. Grandpa's dead."

The tears didn't come immediately. Just a tight, painful feeling in the throat. It took her a moment before she could find her voice.

"How did it happen?"

"He was fishing. And he hooked a big one. And apparently all of a sudden his heart gave out. He was an old man, Susan," her father said. "He really shouldn't have been deep sea fishing at all."

That was right, she thought, Grandpa was an old man. A very old man. In fact, he wasn't really her Grandpa, he was her great-grandfather. He was Colonel Randolph Semmes Hebard, U. S. Marine Corps, Retired, and he was 84.

The General, Major General Randolph Semmes Hebard, Jr., U.S.M.C., was her grandfather.

"Why did the General let him go fishing?" she asked angrily.

"How would you have stopped him, honey?" her father asked. "Grandpa spent most of his life doing precisely what he wanted to do, when he wanted to do it. I think if he'd have been given a choice, this is the way he would have wanted to buy the farm."

"Buy the farm" was a military phrase, a Marine Corps expression which meant to die suddenly. Susan would be the first one in four generations to break the family tradition of entering the Annapolis-Marine Corps. Even her father had done his service before resigning to enter medical school.

"They're going to fly him home right away," Doctor Hebard said. "So I suppose we'd better go home and tell your mother. Are you all right?"

"Sure, I'm all right," she said, but she wasn't, and she started to cry because Grandpa was dead. She remembered very clearly the last time she'd seen him. It had been at the airport when he was on his way to see his son at Camp Pendleton—still tall and erect, with bushy white eyebrows and brush mustache, giving orders to the airline people as if they were all in the Marine Corps. When Grandpa said something people didn't argue with him. The General could no more have stopped him from taking advantage of the deep sea fishing at Camp Pendleton than he could have stopped the moon from rising. Major General or not, he was still the son, and the son just didn't tell the father what to do.

"He was a medical oddity," her father said, as if to himself. "Aside from wounds, he was never sick a day in his life."

When she'd stopped crying, and had blown her nose with her father's handkerchief, they drove home to tell Susan's mother, and to make arrangements for the old man's funeral.

Susan was lying on her bed in her room, still dressed and awake, when her father knocked at her door just after nine that night.

When she told him to come in, he put his head in the doorway and said, "I just got a call from the airport. The General and . . . Grandpa . . . arrive in half an hour. You want to go out with me?"

"Sure," she said, bouncing out of bed. "What about Randy?"

"He said he was already getting ready for bed," her father replied. "I called and asked him."

She decided for the two hundredth time that Randy was a louse. He took after his father, who was in the insurance business and had never been in the Marines. Randy's mother was Susan's aunt, so Susan wasn't surprised to see her waiting at the airport.

There was quite a gathering at the airport. Fairfield was home, and the Hebards had lived there a long time, and Grandpa had known a great many people. And, of course, the Marines were present. The recruiters were on hand, in their dress uniforms, and a platoon from the Marine Corps Reserve, in greens.

Susan stood with her father and her aunt as the plane, a twin-engined turbo-prop with MARINES painted on its side, and a small red plaque with two silver stars under the window identifying it as carrying a Major General, taxied up to the ramp and shut down its engines.

The staircase was rolled out to the door and a young lieutenant in dress blues came out. He was immediately followed by the General, also in blues. The moment the General appeared the platoon from the Marine Corps Reserve was called to attention.

The General came down the stairway and over to where Susan stood. He kissed his daughter and Susan, and then turned to Doctor Hebard.

"I told him that he was too old to carry on the way he was," he said. "Fishing every day, when he wasn't playing golf. Or shooting skeet. He told me that if he wasn't welcome to use my boat, he'd buy his own. I did the best I could with him. Half of my staff got unexpected days off to go fishing with him." He paused. "Doc Labinsky was with him when it happened. There was nothing that could have been done even if he'd been in bed in a hospital."

Half a dozen elderly men came down the steps from the

plane, and took up positions by it. When the flag-covered casket came down the steps, the men snapped to attention and saluted. It was obvious that they had once worn uniforms, too.

Colonel Randolph Semmes Hebard, U.S.M.C., Retired, was buried beside his wife with full military honors the next afternoon in the Fairfield Cemetery. Even Doctor Hebard wore his uniform, a Naval one, because reserve medical personnel for the Marine Corps are members of the Navy.

The Honor Guard fired the traditional three rounds over the grave, and the bugler played taps, and then they all went out to Grandpa's farm, because that seemed the appropriate thing to do.

Susan was a little disturbed when she learned that Grandpa's will was to be read, but then she remembered how often she'd heard the Old Man say that "the time to do something that has to be done is as soon as possible, without fiddle-flapping around."

She realized that as a member of the family she was expected to be present, but she didn't really expect or want anything from Grandpa's estate, and for a long time she really didn't pay much attention to what the lawyer read, until she heard Randy's name mentioned:

"To my beloved great-grandson Randolph Hebard Ward, who is apparently to be entrusted with the sole responsibility of carrying on the family tradition of serving his country [this was obviously a reference to what Grandpa had felt was Doctor Hebard's shameful failure to produce a son for the Marines], in addition to the funds enumerated elsewhere herein for his education, I bequeath my library in its entirety, in the hope that he will find it as valuable as I did in the pursuance of his military career; and all of my sporting firearms except my 20-gauge Browning over-and-under shotgun, serial number 56898 (which is otherwise bequeathed herein) in the hope that they will give him as much pleasure for as many years as they did me."

Susan thought that it was nice of Grandpa to have left Randy all of those guns; they covered one wall of the room in which they sat listening to the will. She looked at Randy and was surprised to see that he didn't look at all pleased. Then she reconsidered and stopped being surprised. Despite his middle name, Randy wasn't like the other men in the family. She had no idea what did interest Randy, but it was neither books nor guns.

She was brought abruptly away from that thought when she heard her own name being read in the lawyer's monotonous voice:

"To my beloved great-granddaughter, Susan Margaret Hebard, I bequeath, in addition to the funds enumerated elsewhere herein for her education, the 20-gauge Browning over-and-under shotgun, serial number 56898, originally the property of her great-grandmother, in the hope that the weapon will permit her to be as good a companion to her eventual husband as her great-grandmother in her long life was to me. Further, I bequeath to my great-granddaughter

Susan my 1947 Cadillac automobile, engine number 47–56756, which I know she has long admired."

Susan felt the tears coming again, and she was bound and determined they wouldn't come where Randy could see them. She got quickly to her feet and walked out of the room. The lawyer stopped reading something about the farm going to Doctor Hebard, and waited impatiently for her to leave.

She went into the kitchen and blew her nose loudly. Only then did she see the half dozen elderly gentlemen who had arrived on the plane with the General. And the young lieutenant, the General's aide-de-camp.

"Anything I can do?" he asked.

"No," Susan said. "Thank you." Then, not knowing really why, she said, "He left me my great-grandmother's old shotgun."

One of the old men snorted, sort of, and said: "Well, if it's the same gun she had in China before the War, it'll still be around when you're a great-grandmother, young woman."

"It's a 20-gauge Browning," Susan said.

"That's it, then," the old man said. "And she was a better shot with it than most men I know are with a 12-bore."

That made Susan smile. Her memories of her great-grandmother were of a fragile (but spirited) old woman who looked like a model for a Mother's Day greeting card. It was difficult, but not quite impossible, to picture her with a shotgun.

"You knew her?"

"I was Old Stone Face's best man when he married her," the old man said. "You bet I knew her."

"Is that what they called him in the Marines?" Susan asked.

"That and some other things we won't repeat in the presence of a lady," another of the old men said. The others laughed. Susan remembered her Grandpa and thought that he would have much preferred to have his family and old friends sitting around laughing in remembering him rather than crying over him.

One of the old men got to his feet, and with a courtly gesture offered her his chair. She was grateful that she had the presence of mind to accept, rather than refuse and remind him that he, too, was an old man like Grandpa.

She stayed in the kitchen with them until the General appeared and issued orders for the drive to the airport and the return to California.

At the airport, Randy did something that confused her. After the plane had taxied away from the terminal, she overheard Randy ask if he could take his mother's car and "go out to the farm. I want to take a look at that car."

His mother stole a quick look at Susan, and said, rather sharply. "There will be enough time for that later."

Susan put it quickly from her mind; she had other things to think about. But it came back to her in the next couple of days, nagging at her. The cold truth was that she didn't trust Randy Ward, first cousin or not.

2

It had always been understood that Doctor Hebard was to inherit the farm, and rather matter-of-factly and "as soon as possible, without fiddle-flapping around" Susan and her family began to move from town out to the farm.

It wasn't really a question of moving. Susan had long ago come to think of the room at the far end of the second floor corridor as "her room." The farm, far more than the house in town, was really home. It was more a matter of disposing of now surplus furniture, putting the house in town up for lease, and moving "home."

On the day that marked the completion of the move, she found herself alone in the house. Her father was at the hospital, and her mother had gone off somewhere.

Susan had uprooted the reflecting sign from the lawn of the old house, and she decided that now was a good time to install it here. She went out to the garage, found a mallet, and carried both sign and mallet down to the road. There already was a sign: It read "COL. R. S. HEBARD, USMC."

She considered leaving it there, and then changed her mind. It seemed to be the height of interior decoration these days to hang up copies of old signs from buses, taverns, and the like. She didn't have a Hope Chest, but she thought it would be nice, if and when she ever got married, to hang this battered old sign on her wall. She uprooted the old one, hammered the "R. S. HEBARD, M.D." sign from the house in town in its place, and walked back to the barn to return the mallet.

She passed the car, and for the first time considered that it was now hers. It was sitting up on concrete blocks, covered with a sheet of canvas. It had been there since the day her father had told Grandpa, "You have every right in the world to drive off a bridge, but you have no right to endanger other people on the highways," and Grandpa had given up his driver's license.

Susan went to the car and jerked the canvas off. A fine layer of dust filled the air and settled on her. It occurred to her that this might not be one of her better ideas, but since she had started, she might as well go through with it. She pulled on the door, and it opened with a squeak. She put her hand on the leather upholstery of the seats and made a visible mark.

Well, she was dirty already. She got in the car and pulled

the door shut. There were 89,504 miles on the speedometer. She tried to blow the horn, but nothing happened. She put her hands on the steering wheel and moved it, until it occurred to her that she was just a little too old to play car driver. The car was huge. She bent and looked at the controls. It wasn't really so old-fashioned, even though it had been Grandpa's "Welcome Home Present to Me," purchased in 1947 when he returned from the Orient and retired, long before Susan was born. It had an automatic transmission, a power top, power windows, and even a power seat and radio antenna.

Whatever it was that worked all these things was apparently worn out or disconnected, because nothing happened when she moved the various controls. That is, not until she pushed the button that controlled the window at her side. The window slid down with a whoosh and this pleased her tremendously.

What the car needed, she decided, was a good bath and a good polish, and the reconnection of whatever it was that made it go. Then it would be ideal for her to use going to school.

She got out of the car then, saw where her seat had made marks on the dust-covered upholstery, brushed some of the dust off her, and closed the door. Then she backed away from the car, appraising it. Even if it had been built before she was born, it wasn't ugly. There was something . . . antique . . . no . . . *classic*, about it. It looked old, but not outmoded.

She was proud of her new possession.

Then she remembered the other thing Grandpa had left her, the shotgun. She picked up the canvas, thinking she would cover the car again, then decided against it. She didn't have her driver's license yet, but that could easily be fixed, and there was no reason to cover up the car again. It was going to be put back into use.

She entered the house, and went into Grandpa's library to the gun rack that covered the wall. Because she was naturally curious, she counted just how many guns Grandpa had had. There were twenty-six in all. Some of them were obviously military firearms. She knew enough to tell the difference between those and a hunting arm, and between a rifle and a shotgun. That enabled her to reduce the number of possibilities to about five guns that could be hers. She finally settled on a gun that was slightly smaller than most of the others, and took it from its place in the rack.

This one had one barrel on top of the other, which fitted the "over-and-under" description, and then she saw *BROWNING BROTHERS, OGDEN, UTAH, USA 20-Gauge* on the barrel. This was obviously the one meant for her. It was a very deep blue, and the rear portion of the metal was engraved with a rather pretty, well-drawn picture of a pheasant in flight and a bird dog pointing at it, with a man about to shoot the pheasant. On the other side was an entirely different picture of two dogs pointing at a bush, and a man holding a shotgun across his chest.

She thought of her great-grandmother, and what that old man (introduced to her in the session in the kitchen as Lt. Colonel Watters) had said about her being a better shot with this than some men. If her great-grandmother had learned how to shoot it, she could, although this might pose something of a problem. Her father wasn't a hunter. She supposed this had something to do with his service in Korea with the Marines. He'd been an infantry officer then, and she supposed he had seen enough of guns then to last him a lifetime. In any event, he never went hunting, and, as far as she knew, didn't even own a gun.

She heard a car in the driveway, looked out, and saw her mother returning. She put the shotgun back in the rack and went out to meet her. The back of the station wagon was loaded with groceries.

"I saw Aunt Marge in the supermarket," her mother said as they carried the groceries into the house. "She said that Randy wants to talk to you, so I asked them for dinner."

"I wonder what he wants?"

"She didn't say, and I didn't ask," her mother said. "But I'm sure, Susan, that you will hear him out with the courtesy he's due as your cousin."

"That's not my fault," Susan said. "You can pick your friends, but you're stuck with your relatives."

"That's just about enough of that," her mother said sharply. And she changed the subject. "I bought a roast. We shouldn't have a party so soon, I suppose, but it is sort of a housewarming."

"I don't think Grandpa would mind at all," Susan said. "He used to say that the only thing wrong with this house was that it was empty."

"You put the groceries away, and I'll start the roast," her mother said.

The Wards arrived while it was still light. Randy, instead of coming into the house with his parents, headed for the barn. That was obviously in connection with his remark at the airport that he wanted to take "a look at the car." Susan decided she would keep her mouth shut until the worst of her suspicions were proven.

Randy's father dominated the dinner conversation. It began with a report of Grandpa's insurance picture and ended up, Susan thought, as a thinly disguised attempt to convince her father that buying more insurance was a virtue right up there with faith, hope, and charity. She envied her father's coolness. He never got excited about anything. The sales pitch just rolled off his shoulders.

After dinner they went into the library for coffee and dessert. Randy went directly to the gun cabinet and picked up a rifle. He worked the action, took a bead out the window, and snapped the trigger.

"You're liable to break a firing pin that way," Doctor Hebard said, sharply.

"What's the difference?" Randy said. "They haven't made ammunition for an old cannon like this since the Spanish-American War."

"You can break it when you get it home," Doctor Hebard said, "but I would appreciate you not breaking it as long as it's still in Grandpa's library."

"Uh . . ." Mr. Ward began. "Randy wanted to talk to you, to Susan . . . about that."

"About what?" Susan asked, looking at Randy.

Randy made a show of putting the old double-rifle back in the case and then picked up the 20-gauge Browning.

"That's mine," Susan said.

"I'm not going to hurt it, Suzie," Randy said.

"I'm not so sure, and don't call me Suzie," she said.

"Susan!" her mother warned.

"Exactly what's on your mind, Randy?" Doctor Hebard said. Randy looked at his mother. He got no help.

"It's your idea, Randy," she said. "You make the offer."

He was obviously disappointed, but shrugged his shoulders and plunged ahead. "It's about the will, Susan," he said. "I've been doing some thinking."

"Is that so?" Susan said. "Do me a favor and put my gun back where it belongs, will you?"

His face colored, but he put it back. Then he turned around and said, "What are you going to do with it, anyway?"

"I don't know, yet," she said.

"The thing is, Suzie . . . Susan," he began, sounding very much like his father, "we have to admit that Grandpa was an old man when he made out that will."

"I suppose he was."

"And what he really wanted to do was make both of us happy, right?"

"I suppose so," she said.

"You know I'm right," Randy said.

"Get to the point," she said impatiently.

"What I'm trying to suggest," Randy said, "is that maybe he didn't give either one of us what we really want, no matter what his intentions were."

"I don't think I'm going to like what's coming next," Susan said, "but go on, Randy."

"Look at it logically," Randy said. "You don't shoot and you don't drive, and you got the only shotgun worth having and the old car." He waited for her to say something, and went on only when it was apparent she wasn't going to open her mouth. "And on the other hand, I was given a library full of books and a collection of unshootable guns. Now, don't misunderstand me, I realize that the books are valuable, and the guns are interesting. Not to shoot with, but just to display, like antiques."

"Those guns are valuable all right," Doctor Hebard said, "in their own right, and as family heirlooms. There's a German Mauser in there Grandpa brought home from Belleau Wood in the First World War and a Japanese Arisaka he brought home from Peleliu in the Second. And there's also a Russian Moisson-Nagant I brought home from Korea and gave him."

"I agree, I agree," Randy said. "The guns belong in the house. That's one of the things I thought about. Susan's liable to inherit this house from you, when the time comes."

"You sound like you're selling insurance," Susan said, and she knew the minute the words were out of her mouth that she'd gone too far. She hadn't meant to, but she'd insulted her uncle.

"I don't think I like that, Susan," Mr. Ward said.

"I didn't mean you," she said. "I'm sorry. Really, I am."

"She has apparently inherited Grandpa's ability to say precisely the wrong thing," Aunt Marge said, with a laugh in her voice that made things easier.

"And the books belong here, too," Randy went on. "They're part of the house, just like the guns."

"If Grandpa thought that, he wouldn't have left them to you," Susan said.

"That's what I mean when I say we have to consider that he was . . . getting on in years, and maybe not thinking very clearly, when he made out his will."

"His mind was as sharp as yours until the day he died," Susan said. "Now, will you stop beating around the bush?"

"Look at it this way, Susan," Randy said. "What you really should have is the books and the guns, and what I really should have is the bird gun and that old wreck."

"What would you do with the car if you had it?" Susan asked.

"Well, frankly, we need a fraternity car. What I'd do with it is take off the fenders and paint it yellow, with the fraternity insignia on the door, and use it for football games and parades and so on."

"Let me get this straight, Randy," Doctor Hebard said. "You're proposing that you give Susan the library and the rest of the guns, and she give you the old car and the Browning. Is that it?"

"That's it," Randy said. "It seems like common sense all around."

"It makes sense to me, Susan," Mrs. Hebard said. "What are you going to do with a shotgun and the old car anyway?"

Randy beamed.

"Flake off, snake eyes," Susan heard herself saying. "That's a lousy swap and you know it."

"Susan!" her mother said, shocked.

"I don't understand you at all, Susan, frankly," Mr. Ward said.

"What do you plan to do with that car, Susan?" her father asked.

"I'm going to make it like new," Susan said. "And drive it."

"Do you have any idea what that would cost?" Randy asked.

"No, but I'll bet you do," Susan answered.

"Where are you going to get the money?" her mother asked.

"I've got almost six hundred dollars," Susan said. "That should be enough to start."

"You just don't need a car like that," Randy said.

"But you do, huh?" she replied.

"I recognize the tone of voice," Aunt Margaret said. "She's not going to part with the car, Randy. You're wasting your breath."

"I think Randy's offer is an absolutely fair one," Mr. Ward said.

"Susan apparently doesn't," Aunt Margaret said. "But I don't think I heard a definite 'no' about the shotgun."

"What'll you take for the shotgun?" Randy asked, immediately.

"It's not up for swap. It was great-grandma's, and I want it."

"I must say I think she's being very unreasonable, Randolph," Mr. Ward said.

Doctor Hebard ignored him. "Let me make a proposal," he said. "Since Randy is apparently uninterested in either the guns or the books, and, as he says, has no need for them, how about selling them to me?"

"They're worth a great deal of money, I'm sure," Mr. Ward said. "Far more than that old car and the one shotgun."

"I'll pay to have them appraised, and I'll pay you whatever price is set," Doctor Hebard said.

"I'll have to think that over," Mr. Ward said.

"It's not your decision," Aunt Margaret said to her husband, sounding very much like Grandpa. "I'm ashamed of the both of you. This isn't a public auction. This is supposed to be within the family. If you'd rather have the money than the books or the guns, Randy, say so."

He hesitated a moment, and then said. "I really don't have any need for them."

"It's settled then," Margaret Hebard Ward said. "You've just sold them to your uncle. And now let's change the subject to something pleasant."

"Perhaps when Susan has time to think it over," her mother said, "she may reconsider."

"I don't think so," Doctor Hebard said. "And I agree with Marge that it's time to change the subject."

But after the Wards had gone home, Doctor Hebard brought the subject up again.

"I think I should tell you, Susan, that when you decide to get married, you'd better plan on eloping."

"What are you talking about?"

"What it's going to cost me to pay Randy would have bought you a very elaborate wedding. You just got your dowry, in other words."

"In other words, you think I was wrong?"

"I didn't say that," her father said. "As a matter of fact, I think Grandpa would have been very proud of you. On the other hand, your mother thinks you're out of your mind, and I suppose you could find a lot of people who would agree with her."

"Including you?"

"No," he said. "Not including me."

Susan would have much preferred to quit her job as a lifeguard. She even came up with a couple of reasons why this seemed to be a sound idea. For one thing, she really hadn't had a vacation. She'd gone to work at the pool a day or two after school had let out, and she thought it only fair that she have a couple of weeks off.

Furthermore, it wouldn't be possible, as it had been from the house in town, to walk or bicycle back and forth to the country club. It was eight miles from the farm to the club.

The two were on opposite sides of the town, and that meant she would have to be delivered to the pool by her father and picked up by her mother (or mooch a ride from one of the boys, something that would irk her pride).

She admitted to herself that these reasons aside, the main reason she wanted to quit was quite selfish. She wanted to get the old Cadillac running, by herself. She went so far as to call one of the driving schools and learned that they would guarantee she would pass the driver's examination for seventy-five dollars, "even," the man said, "if we have to keep giving you lessons from now to Christmas."

It was her money, money she'd earned, and she thought she had every right to spend it as she chose. In this case, she chose to learn how to drive. Then she could get the car running.

Her father none too gently poured cold water on her ambitions.

"You went to a lot of trouble to get that job. Then you took it, and then you started to give lessons to a group of kids who now depend on you. You've got to stay on."

He was right, of course, and she didn't quit. She gave two hours of lessons every morning, and every afternoon, and consoled herself with the knowledge that she wouldn't be spending the money for the driver's course, and so could apply this money, plus the rest of her wages, to the rehabilitation of the Cadillac.

Finally summer was officially over, the pool was closed for the season, and she got her final pay check.

Now she could start to work on the car.

3

The Grand-Roll-Out of the car from the barn came six days later, early on a Saturday morning. Doctor Hebard had come home the night before with a new battery. He blew the horn to announce his arrival, and carried the battery to the barn.

"It's too dark to try it tonight," he said. "We'll have a go at it first thing in the morning. That will be $23.50, please, for the battery."

"Twenty-three dollars and fifty cents?" she asked in disbelief.

"Including tax," Dr. Hebard said. "People who drive luxury cars must expect to pay a little more than those of us who don't. I'll take a check if you don't have the cash handy."

She wrote out the check with some reluctance, consoling herself with the thought that it was more or less a one-time

33

expense; batteries didn't have to be replaced very often.

When she gave him the check (the largest she'd ever written on her still almost new checking account) he laid down the ground rules.

"I'm going to buy the insurance," he said, "because I think you're entitled to transportation back and forth from school, and your driving this car is much more convenient for your mother and me than playing taxicab. I will also up your allowance to cover the gasoline . . . which may, considering the size of your car, prove a major item in the family budget. But the other expenses are yours. I'm doing your future husband a favor. I'm going to teach you that automobiles cost money, and that they are not, like the right to vote, a standard privilege of the female."

"You sound like you're trying to marry me off," she said.

"Not at all," her father said. "Just recognizing my parental responsibilities."

"What if I hadn't gotten the car? Or had swapped it with Randy? What if I didn't have a car, in other words?"

"Then I think I would have helped you buy a car . . . a Volkswagen, an old Volkswagen, and given you the same speech."

"Alice Gunter's father is going to give her a new MG when she gets her license," she said.

"I question Mr. Gunter's wisdom," Doctor Hebard said. "And the cold fact remains that you're my daughter, not his."

"I think I'd rather have you than an MG," Susan said.

"Then you have apparently inherited your father's profound intelligence as well as your mother's good looks," he said.

When they went into the house, Susan's mother said that she'd seen Mr. Ward. "He didn't come right out and say it, but he intimated that Randy is still willing to buy that car, Susan."

"Out of the question," Doctor Hebard said. "Tomorrow that wheeled monster resumes its proper place as the Queen Mary of the local highways."

It didn't happen quite that way.

They went out to the barn first thing in the morning, and as Susan watched, Doctor Hebard filled the battery with distilled water. "A battery stores electrical energy through a chemical process," he said, "a process which involves lead plates and sulphuric acid."

"Oh," she said.

"When the engine is running, it turns a generator, which provides the electrical energy necessary to run the engine; in other words, the juice for the spark on the spark plugs. It also recharges the battery. You still with me?"

"Where did you learn all this?"

"I'm about to run out of the sum total of my knowledge," he said. "Don't be too impressed."

He set the battery aside, opened the trunk, and took out a jack.

"This clever little device is known as a jack," he said. "It is used to raise the wheels off the ground whenever that's ry. When you have a flat tire, for example, or when nt to take a car off blocks."

"Oh," she said.

"I'm a great believer in learn-by-doing," he said. "And there really is no reason why I should develop blisters and calluses and the like working on your car. Your mother wouldn't hold hands with me, for one thing. The jack goes back here."

He showed her where the jack connected with the frame of the car, and watched as she pumped the handle up and down. It wasn't very hard work, since it was only necessary to raise the car about an inch so the concrete block under the springs could be slid out of the way.

By the time she had jacked up all four sides, however, and removed all the blocks, she was sweaty and regretted not having brought gloves with her. But the old convertible was now resting once again on its wheels.

"I'll swap batteries for you," he said, "in deference to the fair sex's alleged weakness. But I want you to watch me, so that you'll at least know what's happening."

He opened the hood and peered inside.

"I was worried about the battery," he said. "When I told Grandpa he was too old to drive, he was so angry that I thought he might forget to disconnect the battery. It would have corroded badly if he had."

"Maybe it's still all right," she said.

"After six years and some months, I'm afraid not," he said, and then he disappeared under the open hood, grunted

36

loudly with the exertion, and came up with the old battery.

"There's a plus and a minus side to every battery," he said, showing her where one of the lead connectors on the new battery had a + stamped on it. "It has to be connected correctly."

Then he picked up the new battery, lowered it in place and tightened the connections. He straightened up and went around to the other side of the car and pulled out the oil dip stick.

"You know what this is?"

"The oil thing," she said.

"How does it work?"

She shrugged her shoulders helplessly, admitting her ignorance.

"You understand the business of the pistons going up and down, don't you?" Doctor Hebard asked. "Or do you?"

"I've got a vague idea," she said.

"OK," he said. "I'll start from scratch. This is a four-cycle engine. There are eight cylinders, each connected to a crankshaft. The pistons fit very closely inside the cylinders. Each cylinder also has two valves, an intake valve and an exhaust valve. The first cycle is when the gasoline, mixed with air in the carburetor and forming a gas, or vapor, is forced into the cylinder, through the intake valve. Then that valve closes. The second cycle is when the piston moves up into the cylinder compressing the gas. That's the compression cycle. When it's all the way up to the top, the spark plug fires, exploding the gas. That's the third cycle.

The force of the explosion forces the piston down the cylinder again. The bottom of the piston has a rod in it, which is connected to the crankshaft that turns. Still with me?"

"I think so," she said. "But you said four cycles."

"The fourth cycle is when the piston is at the bottom of its travel. Then the exhaust valve opens, and the burned gas mixture is forced out of the cylinder into the exhaust."

"OK," she said.

"With just one cylinder going through those motions," Doctor Hebard explained, "you'd get a jolt when the gas was exploded. With two cylinders, you'd have a steadier jolting motion; with six and eight it's pretty smooth. Both Lincoln and Cadillac, by the way, once made 12- and 16-cylinder engines."

"Really?" she asked. "Twice as big as this?"

"The pistons were smaller," he said. "And they found out that there really wasn't much of an improvement in smoothness when they changed over to eight cylinders."

"What's this got to do with that oil thing?"

"Well, the pistons have to fit very tightly in the cylinders. Otherwise the gas explosion would leak around the sides."

"Uh-huh," she said.

"Did you learn about heat expansion in physics?" he asked.

"Things get hot, they get bigger, right?"

"Right. So if you started out with a piston that exactly

fits a cylinder, when the piston got hot, it would expand to the point where it would be too large for the cylinder."

"So what do they do?"

"They put rings around the side of the piston, split rings. which spread out against the cylinder wall."

"Very clever," she said.

"That keeps the piston fitting tightly inside the cylinder, but, since it's rubbing against the side all the time, this brings up the problem of friction. And friction means heat."

"And that's where the oil comes in," she said. "Right?"

"Right," Doctor Hebard said. "There's sort of a reservoir under the crankshaft. The oil is pumped to the top of the engine, where it lubricates the valves, and goes into the cylinder below the top of the piston, so it can lubricate the inside of the cylinder. This 'oil thing,'" he said, showing her the dip stick, "is marked so that you can tell if you have enough oil."

"It looks full," she said. "It's oily up to the 'full' mark."

"That is what I was checking to see," he said. He replaced the dip stick, and then unscrewed the radiator cap. "Go get the hose," he said. "Grandpa apparently drained the water."

She went and came back with the hose. "The engine block is hollow," he said, "and there's a water pump, driven by the engine. The pump forces water through the engine, where it picks up the engine heat. Then the water flows through the radiator where it is cooled by the air forced through the spaces in the radiator by the fan, and by just driving along."

"Fascinating," Susan said, as much to herself as to her father.

Doctor Hebard watched as Susan filled the radiator with the hose.

"Now what?" she asked when she was finished.

"Close the hood and we'll see if it blows up," he said.

"That's all there is to it?"

"Keep your fingers crossed," he said. She reached up and pulled the hood down. It slammed with a satisfying clatter. Doctor Hebard got behind the wheel and Susan got in the other side of the car. She had remembered to wear old jeans and didn't care about the dust on the seat.

The horn blatted loudly, startling her.

"Well, I must have it hooked up right," Doctor Hebard said. "Now the only thing we need are the keys."

"Oh," Susan said. "Where are they?"

"I haven't the foggiest idea," he admitted. They sat helplessly for a moment, and then Doctor Hebard snapped his fingers. He got out of the car, opened the hood, and returned in a moment with a set of keys wrapped in friction tape.

"Spare set," he said. "I wonder why I remembered them?"

He put the key in the ignition. The gauges came to life. The gas tank was full.

"Cross your fingers, honey," he said. He pumped the accelerator and pushed the starter button. The starter whined. And whined. And he pumped the accelerator some more. And the starter whined and whined, and finally he stopped.

"Uh-oh," he said. "It doesn't want to run."

Then he pushed the button again, and the engine caught. It ran roughly and noisily for a moment and then settled down to a reasonably smooth purr.

Father and daughter looked at each other and smiled.

He let the engine idle a moment or two and then released the parking brake and put the gear shift lever in drive. The car started to move. He stepped on the accelerator a little harder and they left the barn.

They had gone thirty feet when the first tire went. It was a blow-out, but it was more of a whooshing noise than a bang.

"Uh-oh," he said. "We seem to have had your first flat."

He pulled on the parking brake and shut off the engine. They got out. The right front tire was completely flat.

"How's your bank balance, Susan?" Doctor Hebard asked.

"It was healthy when I got up this morning," she said.

At that moment, as if in reply, the right rear tire blew.

"What's the matter with those tires?" Susan asked in exasperation.

"They're old and weary, and they have just given up the ghost," her father said. "You're going to have to put new rubber on the car, all around."

He got back in the car and backed into the barn. Susan walked beside it. "Is it all right to drive on flat tires like that?" she asked.

"Those tires are completely shot," he said as he got out of the car. "It didn't make any difference."

"Well, what do we do now?"

"You put that clever little jack back in place, and I'll show you how to change a tire," Doctor Hebard said.

When she had the front tire off the ground, he told her to put the blocks back in place, and then she watched as he forced the tire cover off the tire. He unfastened the tire lugs and pulled the tire off.

"Now it's your turn," he said.

"That's a lot of work," she protested.

"You wanted the car," he said.

"OK, OK," she said.

He had to help her loosen the nuts on the other tires. They had been in place so long that loosening them was simply beyond her strength. He didn't take them completely off, however; he just loosened each one.

Finally, and she was now sweaty and blistered on her hands, all four tires were off the car, and lying on the ground.

"You'd better get the spare out of the trunk," he said. "That'll have to be replaced, too."

"How much do tires cost?" Susan asked.

"I don't really know what tires for this will cost," he said. "But I suppose they'll cost a bit more than the tires on my Buick, or on your mother's station wagon."

"Boy!" she said.

"I'll get the wagon," he said. "And we'll drive downtown and get the tires. Don't forget to bring your checkbook."

She had to go into the house to get the checkbook. Her mother was in the kitchen.

"Where are you going?"

"I have to buy tires for the car," she said.

"Oh, my," her mother said. "I really think you should have taken the opportunity to get rid of that old car, Susan."

"Over my dead body," she said. "All that's wrong with it is that it needs new tires."

"I hope you're right," her mother said, but her tone made it clear she thought Susan was just thinking wishfully.

She learned two things at the tire store. First, that the old Cadillac took the largest size passenger tire normally made; and that tires are priced, more or less, according to their size. The five 9:20 x 15 tires were at the bottom of the price list, where the prices were highest. The tires, including tax, cost her $175.75.

When they got back to the farm, it took her almost an hour to get the tires remounted, and turning the lug-wrench so much broke the blisters on her hands. They stung painfully.

She forced herself to smile, however, and said, "Well, let's see if it runs."

But her father wasn't smiling. "I'm sorry, honey," he said.

"Now what?" she asked, and she realized that she was at once both angry and close to tears.

"Look," he said, and he pointed under the car. There was a puddle of water, with the little rainbows that appear when there is oil mixed with it.

"What's that?" she asked.

"Well, there's more deterioration from long storage," he said. "The rubber water pipes have apparently rotted out."

"Well, how much do they cost?" she asked.

"Not much," he said. "But there's more than that, honey."

"What else?"

He handed her the oil dip stick. It now looked as if it had been dipped in brown, bubbly chocolate.

"What's that?"

"That's what happens when oil gets mixed with water," he said. "The gaskets, which are little pieces of tin and cork or rubber placed between parts of the engine block, have apparently failed. That engine's going to have to be rebuilt, Susan."

"OK," she said, and then her voice broke in rage and frustration. "I'll rebuild it."

"That's going to cost you more money than you have," Doctor Hebard said. "And more, I'm afraid, than it's worth."

"I've still got four hundred dollars," she said, "a little over."

"Well," Doctor Hebard said. "Let's think about it a couple of days, huh? Then you can decide."

"You've just decided to agree with Mother, have you?"

"There's such a thing as throwing good money after bad," he said. "And, to coin a phrase, pride goeth before a fall."

"I'll think of something," she said.

The solution, surprisingly enough, came from Cousin Randolph. He appeared that Sunday night, the day before school was to reopen, armed with the information that the engine needed rebuilding and wearing what Susan considered to be a typical male smirk of superiority.

"I hear you're having a little trouble with the old wreck," he said.

"So?"

"Well, is it true or isn't it?"

"I'm going to have to rebuild the engine," she said.

"You mean, you're going to have to pay someone to rebuild the engine," he corrected her.

"It's still not for sale," she said.

"Don't be foolish," he said. "You can't rebuild that engine yourself and it just isn't worth the price of having someone else do it for you."

"Could you rebuild the engine? I mean by yourself?" she countered.

"Sure, I can," he said. "I took automotive shop my last year of high school. If you know what you're doing, it's not all that hard."

"The answer is still 'no'," she said. "But thanks ever so much for your kind interest."

"Look," he said. "Be reasonable. I'll even buy the tires

and give you five hundred bucks for it, besides. It's worth that much to the fraternity. But they're the only people who would dream of buying an old wreck like that."

"If you want it so badly, then it must be worth having," she said. "I don't regard you as a friend of mankind, Randy."

"Suit yourself, stonehead," he said, and walked away. She wondered if she had been a fool.

4

The Automobile Driving Class at Fairfield High was not a full-term, or even a full-semester, course. The Fairfield High faculty had set up driver training as a half-semester course, and provided four different courses a year.

In a modern-day adaptation of the old trick of dangling a carrot in front of the donkey, students were admitted to the driving courses according to their scholastic standing. Finishing the course meant a 20 per cent reduction in insurance charges, and parents, being aware of this reduction, frequently denied use of the family car to their offspring until they had the class behind them. Often this resulted in a strange and unexpected devotion to studies by many boys in the last report card period before a driving class was to begin.

While Susan never regarded herself as a brain, it was

nonetheless true that she didn't have much trouble with school work, and seemed to have acquired from the men in her family the practical approach to do what had to be done without complaining. She was, in short, in the top 25 per cent of her class.

"Your grades qualify you for the first driver's course this year, Susan," Mrs. Rogers, her class advisor, said. "And I take it you want to take the course in the first half of the semester?"

"Yes, ma'am," Susan said.

Mrs. Rogers chuckled. "You weren't very careful when you filled out your course choice form, were you?"

"I don't know what you mean," Susan replied. Mrs. Rogers handed her the printed card. In the same time period as driver's training, Fairfield High offered several options for those not actually being taught how to drive. For both boys and girls, there was study hall. For the girls, there were two more options, home economics and a typing course that went under the somewhat glamorous title of "secretarial science."

"You put an X in 'automotive shop'," Mrs. Rogers said. Automotive shop was an option for the boys. "You see?"

"That's no mistake, Mrs. Rogers," Susan said.

"It isn't?" Mrs. Rogers said. "You know what that course is? They teach the boys to fix cars. They take cars apart and put them back together again, and it's grease and dirt and that sort of thing,"

"Yes, I know," Susan said. "I've talked to Mr. Fogarty." Mr. Fogarty was the automotive shop instructor.

"And what did Mr. Fogarty say about you taking the course?" Mrs. Rogers asked. Susan didn't reply for a moment, and Mrs. Rogers thought she had won her point: "Susan, what did Mr. Fogarty say?"

"Well, if you insist," Susan said. "He said 'a pretty girl like you down here will probably do away with my class-cutting problem.' "

Mrs. Rogers took a moment to think that over. She tried a new tack: "What will your mother have to say about this?"

"I asked my father," Susan said. "And he said that if it's all right with Mr. Fogarty, it's all right with him."

"I asked about your mother," Mrs. Rogers pursued. "What will she say?"

"I don't think she'll be overjoyed," Susan said. "But she doesn't like the idea of my car, anyway."

"Oh, did your father buy you a car?"

"My great-grandfather left me a car in his will," Susan said. "A 1947 Cadillac."

That was too much for Mrs. Rogers.

"I'll just put a little pencil check in home economics," she said. "In case you change your mind. That's the feminine prerogative, you know."

Susan was driving long before the course came to its official close. As a matter of fact, she was driving long before the class got out from behind the automobile simulators, with their movies of cars in traffic.

She got a little unofficial tutoring from her father, and she practiced a little every day on the dirt roads through the farm, where no driver's license was required since they weren't public highways.

There were five girls in the course, including Alice Gunter, with whom Susan had been going to school since first grade. Alice lost no time in making sure everyone in the class knew that she was going to get an MG just as soon as she got her license.

Whenever a fact was presented, Alice's hand shot up, and she inquired if that fact also applied to MGs, or English sports cars, or cars with four-on-the-floor. It was difficult for Susan to realize that she no longer liked Alice, who had been her friend for so long, but it grew increasingly clear that Alice was becoming, if indeed she wasn't already, one of those offensive people who enjoy showing the have-nots what they don't have.

Alice also seemed to have acquired a new awareness of social position. Since there wasn't much of a social distinction between the students themselves, one senior having just about as much status as another, Alice was forced to acquire her social standing from her father.

Mr. Gunter was the administrator of the hospital. Susan knew what this was, because she'd been curious enough about it to ask her father. His answer had been to the point:

"It's simply a question of specialization and available time," Doctor Hebard said. "There are three general areas of operation in any hospital. The medical function, which consists of diagnosis and treatment including surgery. Then nursing, or caring for the patient under a doctor's supervision. And finally, the operation of the plant itself. The operation of the kitchen, seeing that the hospital is clean, that there are enough clean sheets and instruments and that sort of thing, and most important probably, getting the money to provide the services. For a long time, the chief of staff, or the senior doctor, spent a good deal of his time running the hospital. Then someone had the bright idea to hire a specialist, an administrator, to run the physical plant. It's a special kind of a job, with a great deal of responsibility, and it pays well."

Susan knew Mr. Gunter and liked him. He seemed a pleasant enough man and had always been nice to her when she saw him at the hospital or around town. But she did not think, as Alice Gunter did, that his role at the hospital placed him just beneath old Dr. Hammersmith, the chief of staff, and just above everybody else, including her father and Mrs. Walters, the head nurse.

Alice's attitude was just a minor annoyance to Susan at first, like a small pimple. It grew quickly more annoying as Alice began to make references to the "professional families of the town." So far as Alice was concerned, this category was limited to families headed by a doctor, a lawyer, or a dentist, plus a few exceptions, such as families headed by bankers, a few of the more successful businessmen, and, of course, Fairfield's one and only hospital administrator.

Susan was aware, too, that she was seeing a good deal less of Alice now that she was living at the farm, but when this occurred to her, so did the reason for it. She didn't give it much thought, except to feel a little ashamed at her relief that she was no longer expected to follow the ritual of first stopping for a Coke at the drugstore (and dawdling over it for at least a half hour) and then walking to somebody's house to spend the afternoon on the telephone talking to boys with whom they had just spent the day at school.

She thought she was just as guilty of snobbery as Alice. Alice professed a certain lack of interest with kids whose parents weren't "professional." This was bad, but no worse, Susan thought, than her belief that Alice herself was a royal bore.

The whole business came to a head on the day Susan and the others took the road portion of the driving test. The examination was given at the state police barracks, across town from Fairfield High, and not very far from the farm.

It was a pleasant day, crisp, but not really cold, and Susan had gone out of the waiting room to lean on the brick wall of the building to watch the others being tested.

Alice came out and stood beside her. She obviously had something on her mind, but Susan's first unpleasant suspicion was that she was about to be told again of some characteristic of the MG which Alice would have that very day, presuming she passed the test.

But the MG wasn't what Alice had on her mind.

"And so, on Monday you get out your coveralls and your pliers and wrenches and take automotive shop?" she asked.

"I don't think you start out in coveralls," Susan said.

"Don't you think it's gone far enough, Susan, really?" Alice asked.

"What's gone far enough?"

"You can't be serious about actually taking that course?"

"Well, I am," Susan said.

"Do you really think you should?"

"Why not?" Susan asked. "I already can cook and type, if that's what you mean."

"You know very well what I mean," Alice said.

"No, I don't."

"It doesn't look right," Alice said solemnly.

"What doesn't look right?" Susan asked.

"You, taking that course, with all those . . . would-be gas pumpers and mechanics."

"There's a word for people like you," Susan said. "You spell it Ess En Oh Bee."

Alice didn't say a word. She simply walked away. Susan's initial reaction was of amused tolerance. She almost felt sorry for Alice. If she weren't so pathetic, she'd be comical. Or the other way around.

She didn't really have time to give it much thought. The state policeman in the examination car pulled up a moment or so later, and because there was no one else waiting, Susan was next to be examined.

She passed the test without much trouble and was given a temporary license. The permanent license would be mailed to her. She was able to call home in time to catch her mother before she left, and her mother came to the state police barracks and took her home.

On Monday morning, Mrs. Rogers, her advisor, gave her one more chance to change her mind, but, at five minutes after two that afternoon, Susan Hebard walked into the automotive shop classroom and gave Mr. Fogarty her assignment card.

"Frankly," he said, "I didn't think you'd go through with it, Susan."

"I'm hard-headed," she said.

"Well," he said, "I think it will be interesting for both of us."

"I hope so," she said.

"Well, come on," he said. "I'll introduce you to the rest of your class."

The class, she soon discovered, was divided into two groups. Those who thought that a girl in the class was the greatest idea since the internal combustion engine. Their reasons had nothing whatever to do with automobile mechanics. By far the larger group seemed uneasy, however, as if she had suddenly shown up and claimed a locker in the boys' locker room.

"We teach here by doing, Susan," Mr. Fogarty said. "And as I told you, I wasn't sure you were going to go through with this until I saw you come through the door. Are you still determined to work on your own car?"

"Yes, sir," she said. "That's the whole idea in my taking the course."

"Then the first thing to do is get your car here," he said.

"How do I go about doing that?" she asked.

"Charley!" Mr. Fogarty called out, and a tall, dark, somehow quiet appearing young man walked over to Mr. Fogarty's desk.

"Do you know each other? Can you remember him from all the others you just met?"

She remembered what he looked like; he was somehow different from the others, but she didn't remember his last name, and this showed on her face.

"Susan Hebard, this is Charley Kowalski," Mr. Fogarty said.

"Hi!" Susan said. Charley Kowalski gave her the faintest kind of a smile and nodded his head.

"Susan has to have her car dragged in," Mr. Fogarty said. "How much would that cost her?"

"I'll haul it in," Charley said.

"You sound as if you'll do it for nothing," Mr. Fogarty said. Charley nodded.

"I want to pay my fair share," Susan said. "I don't want any special favors."

"I've got nothing to do anyway," Charley said. "And besides, I'm anxious to see that old convertible up close."

"Words of wisdom, Susan," Mr. Fogarty said. "Don't look a gift horse in the mouth."

"OK," she said. "When do you want to get it?"

"Now's all right with me. OK with you, Mr. Fogarty?"

Mr. Fogarty reached in his desk and came out with the pad of permission-to-be-off-campus passes. He made one out for each of them.

"You got anything else you're taking home with you?" Charley asked her. "No sense you coming back here."

"I've got some books," she said.

"Meet you out in front," he said, and then he walked away.

She had the feeling, and it wasn't entirely comfortable, that Charley Kowalski was being nice to her because she was under Mr. Fogarty's wing, rather than because she was blonde and female.

She got her books from her locker and walked out the front door of the school. Charley was there, at the wheel of a battered and ancient Jeep station wagon, on the door of which was a faded sign "Ski's Auto Wrecking. New and Used Parts."

He leaned across the seat and pushed the door open as she approached. She was relieved to see that he had spread a newspaper over the seat. It was obvious that the wagon was used to haul parts, and that the parts had ranged from slightly cruddy to perfectly filthy. She was, she realized, just a little uneasy.

"You're Ski?" she asked.

"My father's Ski," he said. "But some people call me that. Like all Indians get called 'Chief', it's sort of natural."

"Would you rather I call you Charley, or Ski?" she asked.

"Doesn't make much difference either way," he said, letting out the clutch, and entering traffic with an ease and skill that she was very sensitive to, having just taken a test behind the wheel.

They drove through town to the outskirts, to the fenced-in automobile graveyard she'd passed so many times without giving it a second thought. He stopped the station wagon in front of the quonset hut that was part office and part warehouse and got out.

He walked toward a tall, corrugated metal building, stopped, looked at her, and then gestured impatiently with his hand for her to follow. She gathered up her books and her purse and walked after him. He preceded her and threw open the wide steel doors and then got in the cab of a very large, very red tow truck.

It was obvious that she was expected to get in beside him, something which sounded easier than it was.

For one thing, it was two steps up to the cab, first onto a sort of running board, and then onto a steel step. Negotiating that with an armful of books was difficult. The door, when she had made the second step and was balancing there precariously, seemed to weigh at least two hundred pounds. She was relieved and annoyed at once when he leaned over and pushed it open for her.

This was Susan's first ride in a truck of any sort, and the first time she'd ever been near a tow truck. There was a baffling array of levers and switches and gauges. The steering wheel was huge, and the cab high off the ground.

He turned the key and the engine started with a powerful roar. He reached over and released the parking brake, raced the engine, and then, with a frightening clash of gears, moved the gear shift lever. The tow truck lurched out of its garage.

The ride was rough. It rode, she thought, like a truck, for the first time understanding what the phrase really meant. Charley Kowalski didn't seem at all awed by it, however. As he moved up in the gears, he rolled down the window on his side and rested his arm on the door frame. She realized he knew precisely what he was doing.

On the way out to the farm he stopped for a red light and she felt herself slipping off the seat. He looked at her and without expression said, "Air brakes." She nodded and smiled at him, without the faintest idea of what that meant.

When they turned off the road into the farm, he asked her between gear changes, "Where is it? In that barn?"

Before she could answer, the engine and the gears were roaring again, and she had to shake her head yes rather than actually reply. He wheeled the tow truck around with great skill and backed it up almost to the barn door. Then, with the engine still running, he pulled on the parking brake, opened his door, and got out.

She gathered her books again, pulled and pushed on the door handle, and finally got the door open by slamming it painfully with her shoulder. With something less than feminine grace, she finally managed to get out of, or perhaps off of, the tow truck.

Mrs. Hebard was coming across the yard, wearing a smile Susan recognized as the one she wore when she didn't quite know what was going on.

"What's this?" she asked.

"Mother, this is Charley Kowalski," Susan said. "He's going to haul the car over to school for me."

"How do you do, Mr. Kowalski?" her mother said. Susan realized that she had probably put Charley's appearance together with the fact that he was driving this monster of a tow truck and had come up with the conclusion that Charley wasn't a high school student.

"Hello, Mrs. Hebard," he said, but he didn't pay a lot of attention to her. He got down on his knees and peered under the old convertible.

"Susan, does your father know about this?" Mrs. Hebard asked.

"About what?"

"About you hiring a driver?"

"I'm not hiring him," Susan said. "He's doing it as a favor."

"And where is he going with your car?"

"To school," Susan said. "I'm going to rebuild it in school."

"Oh, I wish you'd given that old thing to Randy," her mother said.

Charley got back in the tow truck, and with a great roar and more clashing of gears, backed the tow truck five feet closer to the nose of the old Cadillac. Then he jumped down again, and began moving levers and switches on the rear of the tow truck. A cable connected to two chains moved off the tow truck's boom, and Charley swung on it with both feet off the ground until it was down as far as he wanted it to be. He took both ends of the chain, which ended in hooks, and fastened them to the frame of the car.

"Do you think you're strong enough to hold this until I take up the slack?" he asked.

Susan went and pulled up on the chains. They were a good deal heavier than they looked. Her hands were going to be greasy and probably blistered again. But she pulled up with all her strength. Behind her, she heard the whir of an engine, and she saw, over her head, the cable begin to wind tight again. She could feel the chain grow taut in her hands.

"Susan, be careful!" Mrs. Hebard said.

"It's tight," Susan said to Charley.

"Taut," he corrected her, and pushed the lever again. Very slowly, the nose of the Cadillac rose and then the wheels, until the car was two and a half or three feet off the ground.

Charley added other chains to keep the car from swinging, and then installed bumpers, half sections of old tires, to keep the nose of the car from rubbing against the back of the tow truck.

"Nice to have met you, Mrs. Hebard," he said. "I'll see you in school," he added to Susan. He got back in the tow truck, slammed his door, released the brake, and with a roar of the engine, dragged the Cadillac out of the barn and down the road toward the street.

Susan admitted that she was very impressed with the way he had done that; she didn't think that very many of the other boys, despite their often-demonstrated ability to make tires squeal when they started off, could handle something as large and complicated as that tow truck with the kind of skill Charley had demonstrated.

She wondered, why it was she had never noticed him around school before.

"I don't really think," her mother said, "that you should accept a service like that as a favor. After all, he must make his living with that tow truck."

"He goes to school with me," Susan said.

Her mother's surprise was mirrored on her face, and she said, "He looks older than that."

He does, Susan agreed mentally. He looks and behaves much more like a man than a boy. Maybe that was why she found him so very interesting.

"What did you say his name was?" her mother pursued.

"Charley," Susan said, "Charles Kowalski."

"He must be one of that family which owns the junk-yard," her mother said. She sounded, Susan thought, like Alice Gunter: not quite approving.

5

"I've got to go downtown again," Susan said.

"Well, I just don't have the time to drive you," her mother said.

"I am the proud possessor of a brand-new temporary driver's license," Susan said. "May I borrow the station wagon?"

"Oh, that's right, isn't it?" her mother said. "Well, certainly. And you can run a few errands for me while you're there," she said.

Driving the station wagon alone for the first time was a thrill, but it wasn't quite as much fun, Susan decided, as driving her own car would be. She knew that getting the old car in running condition would take some time, and consoled herself with the old saw that anything worth having is worth waiting for.

She did four errands for her mother before she did her own. She had to visit four stores before she could find a set of coveralls which were real coveralls, rather than a thin cotton, feminine version of the real thing. There apparently wasn't much of a demand for coveralls to fit someone who wasn't quite five-three in height and who didn't weigh quite 105 pounds.

And the next day, she found that it was necessary for her to change into the coveralls in the girls' locker room, and then walk all the way through the corridors from one end of the school to the other to get to automotive shop. There was more than one snicker behind her back, and more than one reference to her being the new student janitor. But she did her best to suggest that she hadn't heard any of them.

The old Cadillac was inside the shop area, looking dusty and forlorn. But it was there, and it was hers, and she was anxious to get started on it.

Mr. Fogarty showed her the tool room procedure, how to list what tools she required on a form, and how to get them issued. Then he told her that, for openers, she would need a pair of pliers, a screw driver, and a basic set of open-end wrenches.

"Today, I want you to drain the oil from the crankcase, and the water from the radiator and block," he said. "And then, if you have any time left over, you can start removing the water hoses."

"I think I should tell you I haven't the faintest idea where to begin," she said.

He nodded. "Charley," he called. "Will you show her how to drain the oil and water out of that car?"

Charley Kowalski nodded acceptance of the orders, but he was hardly enthusiastic.

"Get yourself a crawler," he said, pointing to what looked like a piece of board on wheels, "and a drain pan." Drain pans, shallow tin pans two feet square, were stacked against a wall.

She got the crawler and the pan and went to the car. She had the crawler awkwardly under one arm, for it was both heavy and dirty, and the drain pan under the other arm. She felt like a fool when she saw Charley effortlessly propel another crawler to the car by pushing it with his foot.

"They're on wheels," he said, quite unnecessarily. "You don't have to pick them up."

"I'll try to remember that," she said.

Charley laid down on his back on the crawler and pushed himself under the car. She laid down and did the same thing. There was no more than two inches between her nose and various parts of the car when she got under it.

"This is the drain for the crankcase oil," he said, pointing to it. "And this little valve here drains the radiator. When the radiator's dry, there are two plugs on the block. You take them out, and the water in the block will drain."

"Got it," she said.

"You sure you can handle it?" he asked, with doubt obvious in his tone.

"Certainly I can," she said. He pushed himself out from

under the car, and then immediately ran the crawler back under it.

"Make sure you have the pan in place first," he said. The implication was clear that she hadn't the sense to figure that out herself. The suggestion was painful because, in fact, she had just been trying to see which of the open-end wrenches fitted the crankcase drain.

She rolled out from under the car, caught hold of the drain pan, and rolled back under, dragging the pan with her. After several false starts, she found the proper-sized wrench and gave a mighty tug at it. Her hand slipped off and smashed painfully into the car frame. The wrench fell with a clatter into the drain pan.

She sucked at the place where the skin had broken for a moment, and then picked up the wrench again. This time her hand didn't slip, but neither did the plug turn. She pushed so hard her shoulders hurt.

Nothing happened. She stopped and got her breath back, and then tried again, this time moving the wrench around so that she was pulling on it, instead of pushing. It began to turn. Very slowly, but moving beyond any question. After three-quarters of a turn, it began to move easily, so easily that she could move it with her fingers.

And then, all of a sudden, it came off in her fingers, followed immediately by what looked like dirty water, and then a darker, thicker fluid, the oil itself. She remembered that oil would float on water. The water that had leaked into the crankcase had sunk to the bottom.

She watched the flow of oil with a great deal of satisfaction. She had done it by herself. She looked at her hand. It was bleeding. She had cut and pulled the skin. She wondered if she would get an infection from the oil.

The oil took a long time to drain out, and then it dripped for an interminable period, so long that she decided that whatever small amount of oil was still in there would have to stay. She replaced the plug, tightened it as far as she could with her fingers, and then wrenched it tight.

She rolled out from under the car, and then got on her hands and knees and reached under the car to pull the drain pan out. It was a good deal heavier than she thought it would be. First it didn't come, and then it came all of a sudden; the water-oil mixture splashed over the end, onto her wrists and the sleeves of the coveralls, and onto the floor.

"You should have asked for help," Mr. Fogarty said behind her. "You'll find the absorbent in a drum by the door."

"The what?"

"The absorbent," he said. "Come on, I'll show you."

The absorbent turned out to be what looked like sawdust, although she was sure that it was far more complicated than sawdust. It was designed to absorb oil and other liquids. It was scattered on the oil, given time to soak the oil up, and then swept up with a broom and a dustpan.

That took her another five minutes. She was able to make a little joke out of it; telling herself that nothing much had really changed in the world. People once swept up stables after horses, and here she was sweeping up a shop after an automobile.

She was surprised, pleasantly surprised, to find that she wasn't being snickered at by the boys. She realized that she probably wasn't the first student to have slopped oil on the floor, that it happened to everybody, and not just to girls.

When she'd poured the contents of the drain pan into a waste drum, she shoved it back under the car, and rolled back under it, no longer quite as awed (maybe frightened?) by being under an automobile. She knew what she was supposed to do next; the only problem was that she couldn't remember where the radiator drain plug was. Charley had showed her, but finding it again took a couple of minutes.

The drain on the radiator was a different kind of a plug from the crankcase drain. This was a nut with wings on it; it was designed to be turned by the fingers. Her fingers, of course, couldn't budge it. She had to hammer awkwardly on it for a couple of minutes with the end of a screw driver before she saw that it was beginning to turn.

When it opened, the water came out with sudden force, splashing her. Then, after a surprisingly short time, it stopped coming out. She remembered putting more water than that in the radiator. Then she remembered that some of the water had leaked past the engine gaskets into the crankcase. She was aware, and somewhat pleased by the awareness, that she now had an inkling of what was going on. She wasn't laboring completely in the dark.

Susan closed the radiator drain valve and propelled herself under the car to the rear of the engine block. The drain there was right where she remembered it to be. It was an effort to start it turning, but she thought she had learned the technique of turning bolts (sort of a steady pressure first, to make sure the wrench wouldn't slip, and then a mighty heave). She tried it, and it worked.

She drained first one side of the block and then the other, and then rolled herself out on the crawler. This time, she applied pressure very carefully and got the drain pan out without slopping its contents over the sides.

She reported the completion of her task to Mr. Fogarty.

"The next thing is to remove all the hoses," he said. "Normally, I'd say just throw them away, Susan, but with a car that old, you may not be able to find the exact part; you may have to have hoses made. Get yourself a box—there's an oil carton over there you can have—and put them in it."

She opened the hood, got her screw driver, and tried to unscrew the devices which held the hose to the connection on the radiator. The screw driver slipped inside her hands. She tried to keep it from slipping by grasping it through a rag, but that didn't work either. Then she had an inspiration. She grasped the handle of the screw driver with her pliers, and that worked.

She just had one of the connectors loose when a bell rang. She looked up at the clock. It wasn't time for the class to be over, but she saw the boys starting to clean up, and after a moment, she realized what was going on. It was necessary to stop work five minutes before class was over to have time to return the tools to the parts room.

The period had gone very quickly. At this rate, it would

take her the rest of the school year to get the old car running again. This was somehow discouraging but, when she thought some more about it, she realized she had accomplished something this first time. She'd taken the first couple of steps, however insignificant they might be.

She got in line to turn her tools into the tool room, and she was now aware that the boys were smiling at her, tolerantly, tongue-in-cheek. If she'd been wearing a dress she would have suspected that her slip was showing.

"Normally," Mr. Fogarty said to her when she'd turned in her tools, "we stay here until the dismissal bell rings, Susan, but I think under the circumstances you can leave as soon as your tools are turned in so that you can clean up."

"Thank you," she said. "It's a long way to the girls' locker room."

He nodded and gave her a funny smile, very much like the ones she'd gotten from the boys.

It wasn't until she got to the locker room, and saw herself in the mirror that she understood the tolerant smiles. She was filthy. She had wiped her oil-soaked fingers across both her forehead and her cheek. The outline of their passage was clearly marked in absorbent. When she looked closer, she saw that she also had a great black gob of grease in her hair.

She looked down at herself. The coveralls were filthy, too, a mixture of absorbent, grease, and oily water.

She unbuttoned them, shrugged out of them, and started to clean herself. She was standing in her underwear in front of the mirror, trying to wash the grease off her face with just-about-useless paper towels when the dismissal bell rang and the locker room was suddenly full of girls, including, of course, Alice Gunter.

"What in the world are you up to?" Alice asked. "You're a mess."

"I wondered what it was," Susan said.

"Susan, you're really out of your mind," Alice said. "You're . . . just. . . ." She apparently couldn't think of precisely what Susan just was, because she shook her head disgustedly and went to her locker.

Susan managed to get her face and hands clean, and to get most of the grease out of her hair (not all of it, however; she would have to wash her hair as soon as she got home). Then she got dressed, and very gingerly picked up the coveralls in her fingers. It wasn't easy, because she had the standard load of books in her other arm, but she finally got out in front of the school, wondering what her mother would say and what she could say in her own defense.

Doctor Hebard, rather than her mother, was waiting for her. He raised one eyebrow when he saw her, and then pushed open the car door for her.

"Wait a minute," he said, "You're not going to ruin my upholstery with those cruddy coveralls." He got out and opened the trunk and held it as she dropped them inside. "Far be it from me to criticize the latest in feminine styles," he said, "but do you really think coveralls will ever catch on?" Before she had a chance to think of something to say

70

in return, he saw the grease in her hair. "You've got grease in your hair," he said.

"Yes, I know," she said, "How come you're the taxi service today?"

He started the car and moved off before replying. "I have just had what is called a heart-to-heart with your mother," he said. "Which, not too unusually, I lost. You're about to get a car."

"I've got a car."

"I think your mother meant one that would carry you from hither to yon," he said. "So I had a long talk with the smiling proprietor of the Chevrolet emporium, and I just gave him a great big check."

"If this means I have to sell Grandpa's car, I don't want it," Susan said, suddenly very angry but not knowing why. "I'll ride a bike back and forth to school."

"Calm down," Doctor Hebard said. "Don't jump to conclusions. I bought this car to please your mother. If and when you get the old car running, we'll sell it."

"Oh," she said.

"It will not be quite as sporty as Alice Gunter's new car —which I saw at the hospital, by the way—but on the other hand, it didn't cost nearly as much."

It was a five-year-old Chevrolet coupe. It had a standard transmission, and there was no radio. But it was a clean car, with a six-cylinder engine that wouldn't burn much gas. It would obviously do what it was intended to do, carry Susan back and forth to school and relieve her mother of that chore.

"There's only one problem," Susan said when the car was turned over to them.

"What's that?"

"I don't know how to drive a car with a clutch and a gear shift."

"Oh," he said. "Well, when I get home I'll show you. You take my car and I'll take this one."

She stopped on the way home and bought two more sets of coveralls . . . all that the store had left in her size. As soon as she got home she put the dirty coveralls in the washing machine and took a long, hot shower. Her hands still looked greasy, and the place where she'd rammed her hand on the frame of the car looked raw and ugly.

Her mother came into her room as she was sitting under the hair dryer doing her homework. She shut it off, as her mother obviously had something to say.

"Don't you think this has gone just about far enough, Susan?" she asked.

"I don't know what you mean," she said.

"I played bridge today, and I must tell you, I didn't think all the remarks made about you being the only girl in the mechanic's class were very funny."

"I don't see anything funny about it either," Susan said.

"I'm trying to be fair and reasonable, Susan," her mother said. "I even went by the Cadillac place, before I spoke with your father, and asked what they would charge to rebuild that old car. They told me first that they'd rather not do it at all, and second that it would cost more than the car is worth just to rebuild the engine, and that's not all that you're going to have to do to it."

"That's why I'm doing it myself in school."

"You're making yourself—and your family, I might add —the butt of all kinds of unpleasant jokes. Do you understand that?"

"I'm going to rebuild that car," Susan said.

"Well, for reasons that are quite beyond me, your father is determined that you should have your chance," her mother said. At that moment she saw Susan's hand. "What on earth did you do to your hand?"

"My hand slipped on a wrench," Susan said.

Her mother shook her head, signifying that the entire world had suddenly gone quite mad, and walked out of the bedroom. Susan snapped the hair dryer switch back on.

In shop the next day Susan managed to remove all the water hoses. There were more of them than she would have thought. And they had deteriorated in a very nasty way. They were rotten in the middle, and they had become sort of glued in place where they had been joined to the cast iron of the block and the brass of the radiator. By the time this session was over, she had the rather large oil carton just about full of odd-shaped, grease-covered water hoses.

She wasn't quite as dirty as she had been the first day, but when the other girls saw her in the locker room with the dirty coveralls and a box full of dirty hoses, she got the same kind of looks she'd gotten the day before when she'd been covered with grease.

At the Cadillac dealers, in the parts department, she got two reactions when she passed over the box and announced she wanted new hoses. The first wasn't very pleasant. The man behind the counter, who was not much older than she was, thought she was pulling a practical joke on him and couldn't believe she was rebuilding a 1947 model convertible. Then the proprietor came in, and very respectfully calling Susan "Miss Hebard," told the parts man that this was "Doctor Hebard's daughter" and sent him looking for hoses that might just possibly be buried somewhere in the rear of the storeroom.

Susan would have been more touched by his concern and courtesy if she hadn't known that the proprietor had high hopes of selling her father a Cadillac to replace the Buick.

After ten minutes the parts man had come up with two hoses. Susan needed eight.

"They just don't make parts for cars that old," he said.

"Well, if I can't get them here, where can I get them?"

"Well, you can try the parts stores, they may have some hoses lying around the way we do, or we can write and ask the factory, or you might . . . you'll probably have to . . . look around the junkyards."

She thanked him, paid him, told him she would pass on his regards to her father, and left. Two weeks ago, she thought, going to a junkyard would have been in the same category as going to the moon. Now she wasn't at all uneasy over the prospect. As a matter of fact, going to one particular junkyard even had a certain appeal for her.

6

By the end of the week Susan had the engine in even smaller parts. She had removed the carburetor and the air cleaner, which was fairly simple. She had loosened, and then removed, the belts that drove the fan and the generator. Then she'd removed the generator. She'd just started to tear the generator down when the warning bell sounded on Friday afternoon.

By then she was almost used to being slightly dirty at that time of day, and had acquired a certain immunity to the snickers and knowing glances she got as she changed from overalls back into a skirt and sweater in the girls' locker room.

Saturday morning after breakfast she took just a few extra pains with her hair and chose her blouse and skirt with just a bit more care than normally. Then she got into the

Chevrolet and drove over to Ski's New and Used Parts.

Charley wasn't there, however, when she walked to the quonset hut. Instead there was a very large, bald-headed man with a shiny face and a large belly.

He looked at her and made the standard masculine scowl of approval.

"Is Charley around?" Susan asked.

"No," the man said. "But he will be. He said you'd probably be over here sometime today. You're Doctor Hebard's daughter, aren't you?"

"That's right."

"I'm Ed Kowalski," the bald, stout man said. "Charley's my kid brother."

"Oh," Susan said. "How do you do?"

"You don't want to sell that car, do you? I'll give you a big one for it."

"I don't want to sell it," Susan said. "What's a big one?"

"A thousand dollars," Ed Kowalski said.

"Are you talking about the car I'm driving, or my car? The old one?"

"I wouldn't give you six little ones for that Chevy," he said. "I'm talking about the old Caddie."

"A thousand dollars?"

"Will you stop trying to turn a quick buck, Ed?" Charley Kowalski asked impatiently as he came from the back of the hut carrying a large, dust-covered book, a manual of some kind.

"Hello, Charley," she said.

"Hi," he said. "There's a method in his madness, Susan. But I told him to lay off you."

"I don't know what you're talking about," Susan said.

"That car of yours is what they call a classic. People collect them, like stamps. If he offered you a thousand dollars for it, he knows where he can resell it for fifteen hundred."

"Twelve-fifty," Ed Kowalski said. "But now that I see the reason for your interest, forget the whole business."

Charley Kowalski flushed bright red. "Will you shut your fat mouth, Ed, before I shut it for you?"

"I'll even tell her where she can sell it. What's wrong with that? Or . . . oh, I see. You want to be the great, big helpful male while she fixes it."

Now Susan was blushing.

"Far be it from me to stand in the way of Cupid's arrow," Ed said. "I admire your taste, kid." He waved at Susan and walked out of the building.

Charley Kowalski finally looked at Susan.

"I'm sorry," he said. "He's got a nutty sense of humor."

"Forget it," Susan said. "Since I started work on the car I've gotten used to people with a nutty sense of humor."

"I sort of thought you'd be over," he said.

"How'd you know?"

"The Cadillac agency called. The boss himself. I suppose he's trying to make Brownie points with your father. Anyway, he said he was looking for hoses for a '47, and there's only one '47 around I know about." He paused. "I told him I didn't have any, and didn't know where I could get any."

"Now what do I do?" she said.

"What I told him has nothing to do with it," Charley said. "We can get hoses for it. That's no problem. What I'm worried about is some of the other parts. Your water pump is shot, for one thing."

"How do you know that?"

"I took a look at it yesterday afternoon," he said.

"Not when I was there," she said.

"Oh, they keep the shop open in the afternoon, and on Saturdays," Charley said. "Keeps the JDs off the streets, I suppose."

"What's a JD?"

"A juvenile delinquent. Don't tell me you never heard the term."

"Are you a JD?"

"I used to be," he said. "Or nearly, anyway. I was a drop-out, which is pretty close."

"But you did go back to school," she said. That explained a number of things, including why he looked older. He was older.

"How long were you out?" she asked.

"Two years," he said. "A long, long two years."

"Original thought," she said. "Better late than never."

He smiled at her. "I thought you would have quit by now," he said. "Especially after Fogarty spread the word that chivalry was out; that you were to get no help from us."

"Did he do that?" Susan asked. "If I didn't know better, I might think he didn't want me in the class."

"You're not supposed to make waves," Charley said. "And you seem to be a natural wave maker."

"I don't mean to be," Susan said. "But I suppose I am."

"That makes two of us, then," he said. "But let me tell you, when you're Polish, as I am, you seem to have a natural talent for it."

"You're back in school for good?" she asked.

"I have nothing in front of me but books, books, and more books for the next five years."

"You're going to college, too?"

"You look surprised. Do I really look that stupid?"

She hadn't meant to insult him, and she knew she had. Then, without really thinking about it, she heard herself say, "I'm surprised. Dropping out and then coming back to finish high school is one thing. Going to college is something else."

"Well, I learned my lesson," he said sarcastically. "The lesson being that you have to play the game unless you really want to be a dishwasher. Or park cars. And then I got . . . sort of a scholarship, to go to college."

"Good for you," she said. She smiled at him, and after a moment he smiled back.

"I'm glad my father, or Ed, didn't throw this away," he said, brandishing the manual.

"What is it?"

"I don't know what they call it properly, but it lists a part's commonalty."

"I don't know what that means," she admitted.

"Not all parts on any particular kind of car are made for that car only," he said, and when he saw that the answer didn't register with her, he rephrased it: "A lot of parts that, for example, General Motors makes," he said, "will also fit Chevrolets and Buicks and Cadillacs; the same part, I mean."

"Oh," she said.

"And the manual tells you which parts are interchangeable," he said. "I suppose that if we were a little neater and a little more organized around here, we'd have thrown this thing away a long time ago."

"I'm glad you didn't," she said.

"So'm I. It's going to come in handy." He paused and seemed hesitant. Then he said, "Have you got anything special to do right now? I mean, if you wanted to, we could go over to the school and work on the car."

"I thought that chivalry was dead," she said. "By order of Mr. Fogarty."

"He was only talking about during school hours," Charley said. "I asked him."

"I don't have a thing to do," she said.

He looked at her. "I guess we'd better go in your car," he said. "The wagon's dirty, and you look too nice to dirty up."

"Sure," she said.

On the way to school she sensed that he didn't think very highly of her driving skill. She was both annoyed and amused. She knew she wasn't a very good driver, but she didn't think her driving was all that bad.

There wasn't much of an opportunity to talk to Charley when they got to the shop. She was surprised to see that he had a key to the tool room and that he apparently had permission to help himself to tools.

"How do you rate that?" she asked.

"I'm spinning my wheels," he said.

"How do you mean that?"

"When I dropped out I was only three subject credits short of graduating. That's just enough to make me go to school full time, but it's not enough to keep me busy. So I decided to take automotive shop. It passes the time, and I sort of get a kick out of teaching the other guys. And girl. Singular."

"That makes you sound like a wise-guy," she said. "A know-it-all. I don't think I like it. You're a student, just like everybody else."

"I didn't say I wasn't a student," he said patiently, sounding something like her father sounded. "The thing is, when I was . . . out of school . . . I was a mechanic. I already know how to rebuild an engine. Or a transmission."

"Oh," she said. "Sorry."

"Do you always go around with a chip on your shoulder like that?" he asked, not waiting for an answer. He disappeared under the open hood with a large socket wrench. She heard him grunt, and then the sound (which she could now recognize) of a stuck bolt finally loosening. In a minute or so he came out from under the hood, bearing a bent pipe which appeared to be made of porcelain.

He seemed to be reading her mind. "They porcelainized

the exhaust manifolds back then," he said. "The same technique you see on some frying pans and pots. They don't do that any more."

He found a place for the part on a shelf on the wall separating this work bay from the next one and went around to the other side of the car and removed the other exhaust manifold.

"Now the heads," he said. "Keep your fingers crossed."

"About what?"

"The condition of the pistons and the rods and the valves," he said. "I'm not at all sure we can buy new pistons for this. If it needs them, and we can't buy new ones, then we'll have to go around and find another junk Cadillac of the same year and pull that engine apart in the hope that its pistons can be used. Valves, we can get. I checked that out in the manual."

She watched him work. The bolts holding the cylinder heads to the engine block were rusted in place. Loosening them took a good deal of strength. She knew that she could never have loosened them herself.

Finally, the last bolt was off. Charley stood up and got a block of wood. He laid this against the cylinder head and rapped it with a hammer. It made a thumping noise. Susan could see where the cylinder head had moved just a fraction of an inch. Charley hit it again, and then, with an effort, took it off. As he lifted it out of the engine compartment, Susan could see where the spark plugs stuck through. She could also see the cylinders and the pistons and the valves. It was the first time she'd ever seen the inside of an engine, and she was pleased that she could recognize at least some of the parts.

It took Charley fifteen minutes to get the cylinder head off the other side of the V-8 engine. Then he took a flashlight and very carefully examined the tops of the cylinders and the cylinder walls.

"I don't think those heads have been off since the day they were first put on," he said. "Look at the carbon." He ran the blade of the screw driver along the top of the piston that was closest to the top. Flakes of black carbon flew into the air.

"None of them appears cracked," he said. "But that doesn't mean much right now. All we can see is the top." She had nothing to say about that, so she kept silent. Charley pointed with the screw driver. "That's where the gasket gave out," he said. "Here and here and here and here. No wonder the crankcase was full of water."

"Is it because it's so old?" she asked.

"That, and the fact that it wasn't used. An engine goes to pieces, it simply degenerates if it's not used. And so do transmissions, which are something we haven't even thought about."

"How do we get the pistons out of there?" she asked.

"You drop the pan . . . that's where the oil drain was, remember?" She nodded, and he went on. "And then you disconnect the rods from the crankshaft. Then they just push out. Since we've torn it down this far, you might as well have the crankshaft ground."

She nodded her agreement, feeling a little uneasy because she really had no idea what he was talking about.

Charley looked at his watch. "There's not much time," he said. "I've got to take over for Ed at one. But there's time to drop the pan, anyway, and maybe take a look at a couple of cylinders."

"I don't want to keep you from anything," she said.

He didn't reply. He laid down on the crawler and rolled under the car. She could hear him grunting, and the sound of the wrench turning, and then the pan, which is a dished-in piece of steel as long as the engine block, came scraping out from under the car.

He said something, but it was muffled and she didn't understand him.

She just happened to be looking at the engine block when all of a sudden one piston came up in the cylinder, seemed to hesitate, and then came out of the cylinder and seemed to fall on its side.

A minute later, another piston came out of its cylinder, and then Charley rolled out from under the car.

"I'm sure of it now," he said. "That's engine's never been torn down before." He ducked under the hood again and examined the pistons and the piston rods carefully, and then said: "These two are all right. We may luck out after all. We'll have to get the rest of them out to be certain, but there's no time for that today."

"If you can't help me in class, how am I going to do that?"

"I figured that out. In class you can tear down the carburetor and the generator and the starter and the other accessories. That'll keep you busy, and then after school, and on Saturdays, I can help you."

"I think I ought to pay you, Charley," she said. "I really do. There's no reason you should do all this for me."

"Well," he said. "Maybe I don't believe that chivalry is dead. And maybe I'm trying to make Brownie points with you."

"You've already made at least three Brownie points," she said. "Large ones, but I . . ."

"How many Brownie points do I have to earn," he asked, very quickly, as if embarrassed, "to get you to go to the movies with me?"

Before she could answer, he hastily added: "I mean the theatre movies, not the passion pit, or drive-in. Just the movies and a hamburger later, maybe."

"Like when?" she asked.

"Like tonight," he said. "Or do you have something else to do?"

"I accept," she said. "And I don't even know what's playing. But I have a condition."

"What's that?"

"That I pay," she said.

"That's ridiculous," he said.

"No more ridiculous than you not letting me pay you for all this work."

He looked at her a moment as he cleaned his hands.

"You're hard-headed, you know that?" he said. "I'll tell you what I'll do. Mechanic's helpers, apprentices, make a buck and a half an hour. I'll take four-fifty for these three hours, and you let me pay for the movie."

"Deal," she said, and put out her hand. He took it. He hadn't gotten all the grease off his hand.

"I can't understand why somebody like you would want to go through with this," he said.

"I can't understand why you're willing to work so hard for a dollar and a half an hour," she replied.

"Well, there's a couple of reasons, and one of them is that I was really curious to see what the insides of that car looked like. Another one is that I admire that old wreck, and I'd like to see it running again."

"What are the others?"

"I refuse to answer that question," he said, "on the grounds that it might make me sound like a fool." He looked at his watch. "Let's get out of here, before Ed has a chance to demonstrate his Polish temper."

When she got home, her mother asked where she had been all morning. She said she had been trying to find parts for the car.

"I hope you don't have a lot for me to do," Susan added. "I've got a date tonight."

"No, nothing at all," her mother said. "Frankly I'm surprised that you found time for a date. You've done nothing except work on the car since school started."

"I suppose that makes me seem like a wallflower, but

this is the first time since school opened I've been asked to go on a date."

"Well, I'm sure you'll have a nice time," her mother said. "You generally do."

Susan didn't quite understand what her mother meant by that remark, but she didn't ask any questions. Since there were no waves, there didn't seem to be much point in trying to make any.

Susan had never been able to accept the rule that the female must always keep the male waiting, simply because she's a female. She was dressed and ready to go half an hour before Charley showed up. She waited for him on the porch, where her father was sitting in Grandpa's rocker with his feet on the porch rail, reading the newspaper.

Charley drove up, right on time, in a Lincoln sedan. It was a beautiful automobile, but when he turned the loop in the driveway Susan saw that the car was missing its right rear fender and the trunk lid. Also a rear door was badly smashed.

Charley was all dressed up, and she thought he looked very nice.

Doctor Hebard put his paper down, took his feet off the rail, and stood up.

"Daddy, this is Charley Kowalski," she said. "Charley, this is my father."

"How do you do, Doctor Hebard?" Charley replied, shaking the Doctor's hand.

"I've got a father-type question to ask, Charley," Doctor

Hebard said. "Were you in the car when that happened?"

"Oh, no," Charley laughed. "We bought that from an insurance company. It was even worse when we got it. A woman from Foley drove it into the Bay Bridge, sidewards."

"You mean you buy wrecked cars, fix them up, and then sell them?"

"Yes, sir," Charley said. "I realize it looks awful but it was the best-looking thing in the yard. It was either this, the Jeep, or the wrecker. Sometimes there's a larger selection."

Mrs. Hebard heard the voices and came out on the porch.

"Whatever happened to your car?" she asked.

"A member of the fair sex," Doctor Hebard said, "drove it sidewards into the Bay Bridge. Charley is responsible for fixing it up, not tearing it down."

"Is it safe?" Mrs. Hebard asked.

"Oh, yes," Charley said. "We don't buy them if there's any structural damage. All she did was tear up the exterior panels. It runs fine."

Mrs. Hebard didn't look at all reassured. "Well, since you're only going as far as the Gunters'," she said. "I suppose it will be all right."

"I beg your pardon?" Susan asked.

"I said that you're not going very far. Only as far as the Gunters'."

"We're not going to the Gunters'," Susan said. "We're going to the movies."

"You're not going to Alice's party? I don't understand."

"That's where I thought you were going too, honey,"

her father said. "I watched them carry the cake out of the hospital bakery. The chef even put a little red MG on top of it."

"I wasn't invited to Alice's party," Susan said. "It's as simple as that."

"I'm sure there's been a misunderstanding," Mrs. Hebard said.

"I don't think so," Susan said. "I don't think Alice quite approves of me any more."

"I'll call Mrs. Gunter right away."

"No, please, Mother," Susan said. "I wasn't invited, and that's that. You stay out of it."

"But you've always gone to her birthday parties," Mrs. Hebard said. "Ever since the Gunters came here."

"And tonight I'm going to the movies with Charley," Susan said. "We won't be late."

Charley was embarrassed, and Susan felt sorry for him. But the movie was a good one, and she was immensely relieved to find that Charley was a member of that small, and splendid, species of mankind who goes to the movies to watch and not to talk or make profound philosophical observations.

Afterward, he gave her a choice between a restaurant or the Crystal Palace, where the fifteen cent hamburgers were the size of a half-dollar, as thin as a dime, and absolutely delicious. They split a dozen between them and consumed two orders of french fried potatoes. Susan had a malted while Charley had a cup of coffee, black.

And she didn't have to wrestle with him in the car, a

fairly standard occurrence with other boys that generally ruined otherwise pleasant dates. Neither did he try to kiss her at the front door.

"I had a good time," he said. "I'm glad you're not a movie-talker."

She laughed with him, and went inside. As she walked up the stairs to her bedroom, she realized that she had had a much better time with Charley than she would have had if she had been invited to Alice's party and had gone. The only thing that bothered her was the feeling that this business of not having been invited to Alice's party was far from over.

7

Susan was one of those people who said "hi" first. But the following Monday, she waited for Alice Gunter to speak first when she saw her in the corridor outside French II, their first class of the day.

Alice walked past her as if she were invisible. Alice was the only one to cut her completely, but the other girls in her old crowd seemed to be somewhat less than overjoyed to see her. Their smiles were weak, and none of them joined her at her cafeteria table at lunch, although she was sure they saw her.

She was being snubbed, or excluded. Susan wasn't sure if she was more hurt because *she* hadn't done anything to hurt them, or more angry. But she was disturbed. She realized that there was nothing she could do about it, short of giving in to the theory that Alice Gunter decided who should be spoken to and who should not, or begging forgiveness for breaking the rules.

That afternoon she tore the carburetor of the Cadillac down piece by piece, and dropped the pieces into a can of solvent which was supposed to cleanse them of twenty-odd years of carbon, gum, and grit. She felt a strange pleasure in taking the carburetor apart. It wasn't difficult physically, and it was interesting to see how all the parts fitted together.

She didn't see anything of Charley that afternoon, or the next. He was on the far side of the shop, tearing down a transmission on an ancient Ford for one of the boys.

But on Wednesday when she walked into shop he was waiting for her.

"If you've got $7.95," he said, "I've got a rebuild kit for that carburetor. Have you finished tearing it down?"

"I finished Monday," she said.

"What did you do yesterday?"

"I took the generator apart," she said. "Mr. Fogarty said the armature must be turned, and I need new brushes."

"You surprise me," Charley said. "I thought you'd still be working on the carburetor."

He put his hand in the can of solvent and came up with a handful of small parts.

"They're still dirty," he said. "I'll get you a brush, and you can clean them. Then, if you're not busy, we can put it back together after school."

"Fine," she said, and smiled, although the prospect of

putting her hands, which had just about recovered from the business of removing hoses, into that solvent for the rest of the period was hardly pleasant.

The reality was as bad as the prospect. When she finished brushing off each small piece and the several large components of the carburetor her hands did not look very much like the soft hands in the television commercials. They looked dry and rough and red, and there was grease and grit under her fingernails.

But rough and dirty hands didn't really seem to be the end of the world, and when she'd washed and rubbed them with lotion, she managed to convince herself that they weren't all that bad looking. She felt a sense of satisfaction in seeing all the parts, now cleaned, lying in rows on a pad of absorbent paper.

She didn't go to the girls' locker room when the warning bell rang. She stayed and waited until the school dismissal bell rang, and then watched Charley assemble the carburetor, using some of the parts she'd cleaned and replacing others, such as the gaskets, from the carburetor rebuild kit. From the speed with which he worked, it was obvious that he knew exactly what he was doing, and she thought about this. It was fairly clear to her that he had not rebuilt many 1947 Cadillac carburetors before, simply because there weren't that many of them around. That meant that most or all carburetors worked pretty much the same way.

She asked questions, and Charley showed her how the gasoline entered the throat of the carburetor from a set of jets in the throat wall and how the gasoline was vaporized by the addition of air as it flowed down the carburetor throat past the butterfly valve.

Finally, much sooner than she would have expected, the carburetor was all back together.

"Now," he said, "if we had an engine to go with it, we could see if it worked."

"What do we do now?" she asked.

"Well, we have to take the generator armature down to an electrical shop and have it ground down, and we have to get carbon brushes for it. That won't take long. If we wanted, we could stop for a hamburger either going or coming."

"Dutch treat?" she asked.

"No," he said. "But we can go in your car, if you like."

"OK," she said, and when they got to her car, and Charley opened the door on the driver's side, she thought for a moment that he wanted to drive. That was a problem, because her father had said, simply and without any fuss, that no one else was to drive the car.

Susan was aware, however, that boys regarded being driven around by girls as some sort of humiliation, and she didn't want to humiliate Charley.

But the problem of what to do never came up. He just held the door open for her, obviously not even considering the possibility that he might drive. She got inside, he closed the door and walked around to the other side.

"Do you mind if I open the window?" he asked. "I like a lot of fresh air."

"Not at all," she said.

They went to the electrical shop first. It was a small, very cluttered shop on a back street behind what was known as "automobile row." The proprietor was a small man, wearing a grease-stained shop smock and an even greasier hat.

He greeted Charley by name, and then, "Who's this? Your girl?"

Charley flushed. "She's a friend of mine," he said.

"I admire your taste in friends," the man said, "although I can't say the same about her."

"You ought to be on television," Charley said. "You're a bona fide wit."

"What can I do for you?" the man asked, undaunted.

"Need an armature ground, and a couple of brushes," Charley said.

"I hope you're not in a great big rush," the man said, gesturing around the small shop. The tables were loaded with other generators, and at least half of these had red tags on them reading "RUSH."

"If I come back in a week, will you have it done?" Charley asked. "Or will I find it at the bottom of a stack of generators, all marked RUSH?"

"Rush I do when I get around to them," the man said. "For you, I'll do it special. Come back in a week."

"OK," Charley said. "Don't fail me."

"Professional courtesy," the man said. He took the generator armature, winked at Susan, and turned back to his work bench.

They went back outside and got into Susan's car.

"He's good," Charley said. "That's why he's so busy. It's not easy finding good workmen."

"You're pretty good," she said, not so much to flatter him, but as a thought that had occurred to her, and which came out of her mouth without thinking about it.

"I'm a competent mechanic," he said, and this was a statement of fact, not boastful.

"Is that what you're going to do when you finish school? Have your own garage?"

"Absolutely not," he said and that fascinated her. Before she could pursue the subject, however, he gestured with his finger for her to pull up at a drive-in hamburger stand, and by the time they'd stopped and ordered, they were talking about something else.

When she dropped him off at school, he asked, "You about ready for another movie?"

"I've got old-fashioned parents," she said. "No dates on school nights."

"Oh," he said.

"But they don't have a rule against gentleman callers," she said.

He looked at her and smiled, "That's not really my style, being either a gentleman or a caller."

She didn't know what to make of this reply, and all of a sudden he was out of the car, had slammed the door after him, and was walking away.

When she got home, her mother was waiting for her with a question. "What took you so long?"

"I had to take my armature down to have it ground," she said.

"I haven't the faintest idea of what you're talking about."

"For the car," Susan said. "It's the thing that makes the electricity."

"Oh," her mother said. Then she asked, "Where did you have to go to do that, or have it done, or whatever?"

"Jerry's Automotive Electrical," Susan said. "It's in the alley behind automobile row."

"It sounds very nice," her mother said, thickly sarcastic. "Just the place for a young girl to go after school alone."

"I didn't go alone," Susan said. "Charley went with me."

"Your friend from the junkyard?"

"My friend from the junkyard," Susan admitted.

"I really don't understand you at all," her mother said. "You've been behaving very oddly since you got that car."

"What have I done wrong? You can't get an armature ground at the country club."

"And you can't get a reputation at the country club, either," her mother said.

"Depends on what you do at either place," Susan said. "My conscience is clear."

"I don't like your tone of voice," her mother said.

"I don't like being accused of something when you've got nothing to base your suspicions on. I went to a business place and then had a hamburger, and I can't see where that's wrong."

"I didn't mean to sound accusing," her mother said, and

she sounded sincere. "It's just that . . . that the other girls don't behave this way."

"The other girls sit around the drugstore making eyes at the boys. Is that what you'd prefer I do?"

"I don't think that's true," Mrs. Hebard said.

"It is, Mother, please believe me. And I'm a little bored with it. I'm learning something. I watched Charley put a carburetor together today. Have you ever seen the inside of a carburetor?"

"No, and I think I could go to my grave without that privilege," Mrs. Hebard said. "What good is this . . . automobile . . . knowledge going to do you?"

"Well, it would come in handy," Susan said, chuckling, "if I ever have to rebuild a carburetor by myself."

Neither really wanted to fight; both accepted the chance to laugh at a joke, however flimsy.

"Let's go make supper," her mother said. "Your father swears that he'll be home on time tonight, for a change."

Mr. Fogarty relaxed the "no help for Susan" ban the next day. He and Charley supervised the removal of the rest of the connecting rods from the crankshaft, and then helped to put the crankshaft onto a dolly. Two of the larger boys helped Charley load the crankshaft into his station wagon and Charley took it downtown to an automotive machine shop to have it ground.

When the pistons and the connecting rods and the camshaft were removed from the cylinders there was nothing left but the block itself, and Susan could look down through the cylinders and see the concrete floor of the workstall.

Susan wasn't surprised when Charley asked her if she'd like to go to the movies again on Friday night.

This time, he showed up at the wheel of a two-tone Ford. But it wasn't two-toned in the regular sense. From the windshield backward, it was light blue, and from the windshield forward, off-white.

"Is that another hybrid wreck?" Doctor Hebard asked when Charley walked up on the porch.

"This is worse than the Lincoln," Charley said. "I don't really know how many wrecks contributed parts to this thing. But at least it's complete and unbent."

Doctor Hebard seemed interested, even fascinated, by the car. Mrs. Hebard, although she didn't say anything, managed to convey the impression that she would have been a good deal happier if Charley had shown up in a car all of one color and that hadn't been wrecked, as if somehow Charley was responsible for other people wrecking cars, and that there was something not quite polite in riding around in one that had been rebuilt.

"What time do you think you'll be home?" Mrs. Hebard asked, not quite succeeding in making it sound like an idle question. She got a sharp look from her husband, and then a quizzical look appeared on his face at Charley's reply.

"The movie's over at 9:55," Charley said. "I figure it will take us just about an hour to have a hamburger or something to eat, which would have us back here within a couple of minutes of eleven. Is that all right with you?"

He had obviously taken the trouble to learn the precise times.

"That's fine," Mrs. Hebard said.

"Susan has sort of an unofficial curfew of midnight—the witching hour," Doctor Hebard said.

"There's not much to do after the movies and getting something to eat," Charley said. "I'll have her home right about eleven."

They were home a good deal earlier than that.

As they passed the theatre, Susan saw two things. First, she saw Alice Gunter in line with Randy at the ticket window, and then she saw the marquee. She'd already seen the picture.

"I've seen that," she said, without thinking about it. She saw Alice nudge Randy with her elbow, and Randy turned to look at the two-tone Ford as they passed by. Neither waved, and Susan thought she saw a look of surprise on both their faces.

"I didn't think to ask you," Charley said.

"I didn't think to ask what it was," Susan said. "What do we do now?"

"Well, I guess you're not hungry," he said, matter of factly. "It's not long after supper. So I suppose I'd better take you home."

"I don't mind seeing it again," she said, "really, I don't."

"I wouldn't ask you to sit through a movie you've already seen," Charley said. He made a right turn and headed back toward the farm.

"I'm sorry, Charley," Susan said.

"Forget it," he said. "It's only a movie."

She asked him to come in when they got back to the farm, but he said he didn't think he'd better.

"Please," she said. "We can watch television, or something."

"You really want me to?"

"Yes," she said, realizing that she really wanted him to come in very much.

Her parents were in the library, watching television.

"Something happen to the car?" her mother asked when she saw them.

"It just looks ugly, Mrs. Hebard," Charley said. "It runs fine. Otherwise, I wouldn't have taken Susan out in it."

"I'd seen the movie," Susan said. "So we decided to come back here and watch television."

"Glad to have you," Doctor Hebard said. "Charley, I hope that you can put up with what my wife feels is my disgusting habit of talking back to cigarette commercials."

Charley smiled, but said nothing. Doctor Hebard saw where Charley's eyes had gone and said, "That's quite a collection, isn't it? It belonged to my grandfather. Are you interested in guns, Charley?"

"Some guns," he said. "I hunt a little, in season. Where'd . . . who was it . . . your grandfather? Where'd he get the Moissan-Nagant?"

"I brought that home from Korea," Doctor Hebard said. "I'm surprised you recognize it."

"Some of the Viet Cong have them," Charley said. "I've seen them before."

"Where?" Mrs. Hebard asked.

"In Viet Nam."

"I didn't know you'd been in the service," Susan said.

"I went in the Army after I'd dropped out of school," Charley said.

Doctor Hebard suddenly got to his feet. "Come and look at them closely Charley," he said. He didn't succeed in shutting off his daughter and wife.

"You were in the service, you say? You don't look that old."

"I'm that old, Mrs. Hebard," Charley replied.

"What did you do in the service, Charley?" Doctor Hebard asked.

"I was the motor sergeant for the 3rd Battalion, 7th Cavalry."

Susan was awed. "Charley, I never knew that. You never said a word."

"That wasn't quite honest of me, was it?" he said. "But on the other hand, I never thought I'd be embarrassed about it, either."

"I don't know what you mean," Susan said. "Why embarrassed?"

"Just how old are you, Charley?" Mrs. Hebard asked, and now there was no attempt to make it an idle question.

She sounded like the district attorney questioning a suspected murderer.

"Age is sort of relative, Mrs. Hebard," Charley said. "I was old enough to be a sergeant, and that's what I think you're driving at." He looked at Susan for just a moment and then said, "I'll be going now. Good night, Doctor. Good night, Mrs. Hebard. Susan."

"Why are you leaving?" Susan said. "What happened that I missed?"

"Good night," Charley said again, and then he was gone.

"Will somebody please tell me what happened? What was that all about?"

"I think the point your mother is making, is that Charley is just a little too old for you," Doctor Hebard said.

"You don't agree with me?" Mrs. Hebard challenged.

"I don't know how old he is; he didn't say," Doctor Hebard said.

"He was old enough to be in the Army, and that makes him too old for Susan," Mrs. Hebard said, "It's as simple as that."

"I had some seventeen-year-olds in my company in Korea that I would be delighted to have Susan go out with," Doctor Hebard said. "And from what I saw of that young man, he's all right."

"No wonder Alice didn't invite Susan to her party," Mrs. Hebard said. "I can't say that I blame her."

"Susan, I think you'd better go to your room," Doctor Hebard said. "Your mother and I are about to have an argument, and I read somewhere that hearing their parents fight sends impressionable young girls straight to the psychiatrist's couch."

"There's nothing whatever to argue about," Mrs. Hebard said. "Susan has seen the last of that boy, or that man, and that's that."

"Go on up to your room, Susan," Doctor Hebard said.

"I think I'd prefer to stay, rather than have you talk behind my back."

"I didn't ask you what you'd prefer," her father said angrily. "Now get out of here before I really get mad at you."

She obeyed, and she got as far as the mirror in her bathroom before she started to cry. That made her mad, and the madder she got, the more she cried.

8

At breakfast the next morning Doctor Hebard was dressed in a cotton plaid shirt and a button sweater, rather than his standard white shirt and tie, and Susan knew he wasn't going to the office. She sensed that the reason he wasn't going to the office was directly connected with what had happened the night before.

Breakfast was awkward. Mrs. Hebard was tight-lipped; Doctor Hebard read the newspaper from cover to cover. Then all of a sudden he said, "Let's take a walk, Susan. Are you dressed warmly enough?"

"I'll put a sweater on," she said.

"Why the sudden interest in walking?" she asked when she came back to the kitchen.

"I found out a long time ago that I think better in the open air," he said. "I don't know why, but that's the way it is. Indulge me, honey."

Susan understood that her father stood in the middle of the battle between her mother and her. She was fairly sure that in a showdown, he'd take her mother's side, but she also knew that, above all, her father had a sense of what was fair.

They walked out behind the barn and into the fields before he spoke.

"When your mother went down to the road to get the newspaper this morning," he said, "I had a telephone call."

"Oh?"

"From your Aunt Marge," he said.

"What did she want?"

"I think she would have preferred not to call at all," Doctor Hebard said. "But she decided it was more a case of her duty to me as my sister and your aunt, than of being a carrier of tales."

"What sort of tales?" Susan asked, with a sick feeling in her stomach.

"Your Cousin Randy apparently has a new ladylove," Doctor Hebard said. "Your friend Alice Gunter."

"She's no friend of mine," Susan said.

"Not as you and I understand the word, she isn't," Doctor Hebard agreed. "She's apparently decided that circumstances make friends, rather than anything else."

"What do you mean by that?"

"Well, because her father and I both work at the hospital, and because she's going out with Randy, you simply have to be friends."

"Not in my book," Susan said.

"Let me finish," Doctor Hebard said. "Aunt Marge told me somewhat reluctantly what Randy had told her."

"Which was?"

"That he and Alice were standing in front of the movies last night; that you and Charley drove by, saw them, and kept going. The implication being that you kept going to some place you shouldn't have been going to, some place where you didn't want anyone to see you."

"That dirty-minded louse!" Susan exploded. "Both of them! You know very well where we went last night, and how long it takes to go to the movie from the farm and back again."

"Yes, I do, and I told Marge so."

"What did she say then?"

"Well, I don't know if you'll believe this or not, but she was very happy to be wrong."

"I should hope so," Susan said.

"The thing you're going to have to keep in mind, honey," he said, "is that there are least three people on your side—me, your mother, and Aunt Marge."

She could think of only one reply to that, one which would sound fresh and probably was fresh, and would make her father mad, so she said nothing.

"With that in mind—and she was sincere, Susan, really— she asked me what 'all the talk about you and Charley is all about.'"

"What did you say?"

"I told her I didn't know what talk she was talking about, and didn't particularly care to listen to nasty gossip."

"Thanks."

"But that doesn't help things much, I'm afraid," Doctor Hebard said. "Apparently there is some talk."

"I don't know why there should be," Susan said. "I haven't done anything wrong."

"You've committed the cardinal sin," Doctor Hebard said.

"What do you mean by that?"

"You've behaved differently."

"Is that wrong? I mean, if I'm not doing anything wrong, why is it wrong?"

"The world isn't always fair and just. The point your mother made, unfortunately, is a valid one."

"What point did she make?"

"That your association with Charley is damaging your reputation."

"Baloney!" Susan said. "And so what if it is?"

"If I had been asked," he said, wryly, "I could have predicted that answer. First of all, honey, it's not baloney. If Aunt Marge is concerned enough to call me, then it's not baloney."

"Charley's a very nice guy," Susan said. "And all he's done is help me with the car, and take me to the movies. He's never tried to hold my hand, much less kiss me or anything."

"The cold hard fact is that you're seventeen, Susan.

Charley is older than that, old enough to have served in Viet Nam, after having dropped out of school."

"You forgot that his family owns the junkyard. That's certainly a valid argument for the other side."

"Well, it wouldn't be with me," Doctor Hebard said sharply. "Nor with your mother, once she had a chance to get used to the idea."

"Is Charley supposed to be ashamed about being a sergeant in Viet Nam?"

"No, and I made that same point in my . . . discussion . . . of this matter with your mother last night. In the Marines—and I'm sure the Army is very much the same way—you don't get to be a sergeant unless you've demonstrated certain admirable traits of character. Particularly if you're as young as Charley is."

"You just said he was so old," she argued.

"Two or three years' difference at your time of life is a much greater difference than it is when you're forty. Or even twenty-odd," Doctor Hebard said. She didn't like it, but she knew he was right.

"There are two things that really bother your mother, Susan," he said, "And they bother me, too, to be perfectly honest."

"What are they?"

"She's primarily concerned for your welfare. When you get right down to it, Charley is the first boy . . . man, if you like . . . that you've ever felt strongly about."

"It's not like that at all," Susan protested. "He's never so much as tried to hold my hand. I told you that. Which is probably why I like to be with him. I don't have to spend all my time fighting him off."

"In the eyes of people like Randy, I'm afraid, it looks like Charley is a widely experienced wrestler, taking advantage of a young girl."

"Well, that's not true, and I don't really care what Randy thinks."

"It's not that black and white, honey, I'm afraid."

"Just what did you and Mother decide last night?"

"Only that I would have a 'talk with you,'" he said. "That's what I'm doing."

"We seem to be at a dead end, if you were supposed to convince me of the error of my ways," Susan said. "Since I haven't done anything wrong, I can hardly promise not to do it again."

He laughed. "Have you ever considered being a lawyer . . . for the defense?"

"I have the strength of ten," she said, "because—no joke —in my heart, I'm pure."

"I know," he said, chuckling.

"You didn't tell me what happened, or what great decision has been made."

"Nothing spectacular," Doctor Hebard said. "Nothing you can't live with, I don't think. As I started to say a moment ago, the major problem, at least in your mother's and your aunt's eyes, is that you're seeing too much of Charley. Seeing him exclusively, in other words."

"I've been out with him twice," she protested. "Just

twice. And the second time, we weren't gone thirty minutes."

"But you have been running around automobile row with him."

"And what's wrong with that?"

"Your mother thinks it looks bad, and I'm not so sure she's wrong."

She said nothing.

"She thinks . . . we think . . . that you should give the other boys a chance. Being very specific, you can go out with Charley every third date you have."

She giggled. That was ridiculous.

"And you are not to go out to either the junkyard, or to automobile row, or to the Automotive Shop after school or on weekends," Doctor Hebard added.

"That's all?" she asked.

"That's all."

"I can live with that," she said. "I think you're silly, but if that's the way you want it, it's OK with me."

"It's a lot better than being chained up in the castle tower, Princess," her father said, laughing with her.

"There's one thing you and Mother have overlooked," Susan said.

"What's that?"

"You seem to have the idea that the boys are standing in line to ask me for a date. That just isn't so."

"Oh, I don't think that will be a problem," her father said. "If I were seventeen or eighteen, I'd try to take you out."

"But you're smart," she said, and it was half a joke and half serious, "which is more than I can say for most of the boys I know."

He raised his eyebrows and looked as if he was going to say something, and then apparently changed his mind. It was obvious that he was purposely changing the subject when he said: "I thought this was going to take a good deal longer than it did. I don't feel like going to work now, especially since I'm not expected there. How shall we spend the morning? Got any ideas?"

"Not a one. But let's think of something."

"This is the kind of weather Grandpa called shooting weather," he said. "Brisk, and clear. A good time to be out of doors."

"What shall we shoot?" she asked.

"Season's not open," he said. "That limits things somewhat." He paused. "What do you say we go down to the hardware store and buy a box of pigeons and teach you how to shoot the 20-bore?"

"Do you want to?"

"Yes," he said. "I guess I do. For the first time in a long time, I think it would be fun."

"Let's do it then."

They walked back to the barn and got in the Buick and drove downtown to the hardware store.

"I'm sorry, Doctor," the proprietor said. "I stopped stocking clay birds about a year ago when the gun club opened. I guess you could buy some out there."

"Let's call and find out," Doctor Hebard said.

"I'll be glad to call for you," the proprietor said, and he went in the back room of the hardware store. He came back out in a minute or two. "They said they'd be glad to have you," he said. "As a matter of fact, Doctor, I spoke with Doctor Maroney. He said to tell you the club's as good a place as any for your pressing personal business. I don't know what he meant by that, but he said to give you that message."

"I know what he means," Doctor Hebard said. "Thank you."

"What was that all about?" Susan asked when they got back in the car.

"Oh, Maroney was there when I told Doctor Phillips I wouldn't be in this morning, because of 'pressing personal business,' " Doctor Hebard said.

"Oh, I got you in trouble, didn't I?" Susan asked. "I'm sorry, Dad."

"No trouble," her father said. "I've filled in too many times for Phillips when he went fishing to be the slightest bit embarrassed." He paused. "I'd forgotten that Maroney was a shooter. I should have remembered. I was asked to join when they first formed the club."

"Is that the place out past the farm?"

"Uh-huh," her father said. "We might as well stop by the house and pick up the guns. It would be simpler than going out there and buying birds."

The gun club turned out to be a small concrete block

clubhouse with two fields behind it, one for skeet shooting and the other for trap. A dozen cars were parked by the clubhouse, and by the identifying medallions on several license plates, Susan saw that Doctor Maroney wasn't the only other doctor present.

Her father pushed the door open ahead of her and she walked inside the small building. She recognized Doctor Maroney immediately, and then, a moment later, his son. He looked very much like his father, but the last time she'd seen him, four or five years earlier, before Doctor and Mrs. Maroney had been divorced and she had moved away with the boy, he'd been more or less a runt. He's grown, she thought.

"Hello, Susan," Doctor Maroney said, "and good morning to you, Doctor. This is your pressing business, I presume?"

"Hello, Al," Doctor Hebard said. "People who live in glass houses, and so on."

Maroney laughed.

"And I confess that Susan is my pressing business," Doctor Hebard added.

"Hello, Susan," Ted Maroney said. "Remember me?"

"You've grown," Susan said.

"So've you," he said with a smile.

"Ted's over at the University," Doctor Maroney said as Ted shook hands with Doctor Hebard. "He gets over a couple of times a month."

"It's nice to see you again, Ted," Doctor Hebard said. "Are you a shooter?"

114

"I think he comes over here to shoot up my shells, rather than just to pass time with Dear Old Dad," Doctor Maroney said, his smile making it gentle.

"You're a freshman now, Ted?" Doctor Hebard asked.

"Sophomore," Ted answered.

"I didn't know you were a skeet shooter, Susan," Ted went on. It was interesting, even flattering, to see his interest in her as a female.

"I'm not," she said. "I've never fired a shotgun in my life."

"I figured it was high time," Doctor Hebard said. "That's why we're here."

"We're glad to have you," Doctor Maroney said. "We can use the money. And I'm sure there's a gun around here for Susan."

"She's got one," Doctor Hebard said. "A Browning over-and-under."

"That's the way to start, first class," Ted Maroney said.

"I inherited it from my great-grandfather," Susan said.

"You ever shoot any skeet, Randy?" Doctor Maroney asked.

"Not since I was in the service," Doctor Hebard said.

"My favorite sport is watching television," Doctor Maroney said. "But my wife cruelly suggests that I get fat doing that. She insists that I get out in the great outdoors, and I find that skeet's much more interesting than hitting at a small white ball with a weighted stick."

"Are you any better at hitting these clay pigeons?" Doctor Hebard asked, straight-faced. "I know you have trouble with golf balls."

"I'll show you," Doctor Maroney said. "Susan might as well see how an expert does it."

They went outside to the car and got their guns, and then walked to the first station of the skeet field. Susan was shown how the safety and barrel selector on her gun worked, and then watched as Doctor Maroney called for a bird.

When he yelled "pull," a small round clay target came flying out of the building beside him. When it was fifteen yards or so away, Doctor Maroney fired at it, and it shattered into a cloud of black dust.

Then he called "pull" again, and a target flew out of the house at the far side of the half-circle range, headed almost directly at him. He waited until it was almost up to him before firing and breaking it.

"I realize that's asking a good deal of someone who has your slow reflexes, Randy," Doctor Maroney said to Doctor Hebard. "So we'll understand when you miss."

"Can I have one practice shot before you start counting?" Doctor Hebard asked.

"Help yourself."

"How about two practice shots?" Doctor Hebard asked.

"Anything to help you with your pressing personal business," Doctor Maroney said.

Doctor Hebard loaded two shells into his shotgun, a Model 12 Winchester pump.

"Anytime you're ready, Doctor," Doctor Maroney said.

"Pull me doubles," Doctor Hebard said, without putting the gun to his shoulder.

"Aren't you going to mount the gun?" Doctor Maroney said.

"That's for beginners," Doctor Hebard said. "Pull doubles, Charley. *Pull.*"

Susan heard the machine that threw the targets whirl, and then she saw that a target had been thrown simultaneously from each house. There was a target going away, and one coming in.

Moving with deceptive slowness her father put the shotgun to his shoulder and in one smooth movement fired and broke the target going away, and then worked the action, ejecting the fired shell, loaded a fresh one, and fired and broke the incoming bird.

"Where have you been shooting?" Doctor Maroney asked. "Not here. And the nearest other club's over in Farmington."

"It's like a bicycle," Doctor Hebard said. "Once you learn to do it with a certain undeniable flair, you never forget how."

Ted Maroney took his position, and called for his birds, one at a time, and broke both.

Then it was Susan's turn.

She took up her position, loaded the gun, and making sure the safety had been released, put it to her shoulder. "Pull!"

She barely saw the bird. By the time her eyes found it, it was more than halfway across the semicircle, and she wasn't surprised that it continued its flight untouched after she fired at it.

"Try it again," Doctor Hebard said. "Shoot as quick as you can, and just a little bit under it."

"Pull!" she called again. She fired. To her surprise, the bird broke.

"That's the way," her father said. "Now you get a low house. Shoot just a couple of inches in front of it, and wait until it gets almost to you."

She missed the low house.

They moved to the next station. Again the men broke both of their targets. She missed both, and then Ted broke both of his. Susan could see that Doctor Maroney was just a little bit disturbed at the effortless skill with which her father shot.

Neither man said anything, however, until they'd completed the seven stations making up the semicircle. Then, at the station in the center, where the birds flew almost directly over the shooter's head, Doctor Maroney missed.

"I hope your reflexes are in better shape when you're in the operating room, Doctor," Doctor Hebard said tolerantly. He called for his birds and broke both, without any apparent effort.

"OK, Randy," Maroney said. "I bite. Where did you learn how to shoot?"

"One time my company had to guard a First Marine Air Wing airfield for three months. I lived in a tent with some of the pilots. They were issued all the shotgun shells they could shoot, so they would have a sharp eye for aerial gunnery. I had nothing else to do but shoot skeet and check the guard posts. I got pretty good at it."

"I knew there had to be some crooked answer," Doctor Maroney said.

"I'd forgotten how much fun it is," Doctor Hebard said. "I'll have to come out here more often."

"I wish you'd teach me," Susan said, "I've only hit four of them."

"I'll teach you," Ted said very quickly.

"I accept your offer," Doctor Hebard said as quickly. "I adhere to that sound principle that you learn better from people outside the family. I taught Susan's mother how to drive. It was a painful experience."

Susan wondered if he meant that, or whether she was being thrown at Ted Maroney. After all, Ted was Doctor Maroney's boy, and Mrs. Hebard liked Mrs. Maroney. Ted hadn't dropped out of school, and he didn't work in a junkyard.

Then she was ashamed of herself. Her father wasn't that type. She was honest enough to admit to herself that the reason she had brought up the boy-girl business was that Ted was a very unusual specimen of the male species.

"I agree with you, Dad," she said. Ted Maroney smiled.

They returned to the first two and the last two stations on the semicircle and fired at double targets, thus finishing the round. Then her father and Doctor Maroney went into the clubhouse, while she was led back to the first station by Ted, who matter-of-factly began to instruct her.

9

"How did she do?" Doctor Hebard asked thirty minutes later when they walked into the clubhouse.

"Not bad at all," Ted Maroney said approvingly. "She's got a feeling for it."

"It's fun," Susan said. She was not being polite. It had been fun. There had been none of the recoil, none of the smoke, that she had thought would come with firing a shotgun. It was a matter of skill, of precision of eye, of quick reaction. It was very much like shooting free baskets in basketball, but much more interesting. She thought she knew why Doctor Maroney prefered skeet shooting to golf.

"Is she good enough to take on her father?" Doctor Hebard asked. "I promised to give this tired old man some lessons myself."

"I'm tired," Susan said, thinking out loud. "But I'd love to try a whole round again. All we did was practice."

"Well, then, let's shoot one more before I take you home and show you the unpleasant side of this sport."

"What's the unpleasant side?"

"Cleaning the guns," Doctor Hebard said. "And since I'm paying for the shells, it seems to me that you've inherited that responsibility."

"That's fair," Susan said.

The competition turned out to be between Doctor Hebard and Ted. Doctor Maroney missed three birds before reaching the center station. Susan had reached the point where she knew at the time she pulled the trigger whether or not she was going to hit the bird, and she sensed this was a major step toward becoming a decent shot.

Doctor Hebard missed one of his first pair of doubles, and Ted got as far as the last station on doubles before he too missed. They had tied each other, breaking twenty-four out of twenty-five.

Susan loyally decided that made her father the better shot; he hadn't shot a gun in years and he did as well as Ted, who apparently shot all the time and much better than Doctor Maroney.

She'd broken eleven, which was far from spectacular, but she decided that was eight or nine more than she had any right to expect she'd break.

When they were gathered around the score card, Ted said to her, "A few more lessons and we'll make a skeet shooter out of you. Eleven isn't bad."

"An inherited skill," Doctor Hebard said. "Blood tells.

You must take after your mother, Ted. Your reflexes are in pretty good shape."

"I don't think I like him," Doctor Maroney said. "It reminds me of what we used to say in the Army about always being able to tell a Marine. But not much."

They all laughed, and then Ted caught Susan off balance.

"If you'll go to a party with me tonight, Deadeye," he said, "I could be talked into picking you up early and cleaning that gun for you."

From the look on her father's face, Susan saw that he was as surprised at the invitation as she was. He looked at her to see what she would do.

"I think I'd like to clean it myself," she said. "But I am free this evening."

"You can come by early and clean mine, Ted," Doctor Hebard said. "As a matter of fact, I'll even arrange to feed this lousy shot you call your father, if you want."

"We were going to have dinner at the country club," Doctor Maroney said. "But on behalf of my son, we accept. I dearly love home-cooked food, especially if it's free."

"It's settled then," Doctor Hebard said. "We'll see you about six?"

On the way home, Doctor Hebard said, "I have something to say, but in view of our previous conversation, I don't know whether I should or not."

"What's that?"

"Ted Maroney is a nice young man."

"Yes, he is."

"I didn't know he was going to be out there," Doctor Hebard said.

"I'm glad he was," Susan said. "And I'm glad we went. I really enjoyed that."

"I take it you'd be willing to go back?"

"If you twist my arm a little," she said.

Mrs. Hebard was sitting at the kitchen table waiting for them when they got home.

"You were certainly gone long enough," she said.

"What's the condition of the family larder?" Doctor Hebard asked.

"Why do you ask?"

"We're having guests for dinner," he said. "Al Maroney. And Ted."

"Oh?"

"And then Ted's taking Susan to a party," Doctor Hebard said.

"Oh, how nice," she said. She was visibly pleased. "I'll have to get a roast or something right away. I suppose both of them could use a good home-cooked meal."

The Maroneys arrived on time, and in two cars. Doctor Maroney was driving his car, an Oldsmobile, and Ted was at the wheel of a fire-engine red Fiat Spider convertible.

"What a pretty little car," Mrs. Hebard said when they walked up on the porch.

"In the interest of fair play, and to keep you from accusing me of being an overly indulgent parent, Phyllis," Doctor Maroney said, "and because I'm proud as punch about it, Ted bought that red machine with his own money. He's in Naval ROTC, and they not only pay his tuition, but give him $50 a month besides, and pay him during the summer when he goes off for training."

Mrs. Hebard beamed, and then looked at Susan as if to make sure she had heard, understood, and appreciated what a splendid young man Ted Maroney was. Ted looked distinctly uncomfortable.

"I promised to clean your gun," he said. "You want to show me where it is?"

"In the library," Doctor Hebard said. "The cleaning stuff's in a drawer under the rack."

Susan led Ted into the library. He was impressed with the collection of guns and said so. He pulled open the drawer beneath the rack of guns and smiled.

"Why the smile?"

"I wondered how you were supposed to clean a gun in here without making things dirty," he said, "and now I know." He came up with a roll of old carpeting. It just fit the large table next to the rack.

"Grandpa must have figured that out," she said. "He was quite a guy."

"Whatever happened to that old convertible of his?" Ted asked.

"I've got it," she said. "I'm having it rebuilt in school."

"Good for you," he said, obviously delighted.

"A boy named Kowalski's helping me with it," Susan said, giving in to a compulsion to somehow bring Charley's name up.

"Charley Kowalski, by any chance?" Ted asked.

"You know him?"

"Sure. I practically grew up with him. What's he still doing in high school?"

"He dropped out and then came back," she said, making it almost a challenge.

"He never struck me as the dropout type," Ted said. "We used to be pretty good buddies, before my parents were divorced and I moved away."

"He's a very nice guy," Susan said.

"You make that sound like a challenge," Ted said.

"I didn't mean to," she said, slightly embarrassed that he had sensed this.

Ted had taken off his coat and now he neatly rolled up his sleeves. "I suppose there's solvent and a rod and a brush in here," he said, looking into the drawer again and coming up with the cleaning equipment.

He took the gun apart and then handed her the barrels. "Look at the light through them," he ordered. "See the streaks?"

"Uh-huh. What are they?" she asked.

"Lead. The barrel looks smooth, but it's really rough enough to scrape tiny pieces of lead off each individual shot."

"This may sound stupid, but what's the difference? What happens if you don't clean it off?"

"Moisture collects underneath it, between the lead and the barrel, and that rusts."

"Oh," she said.

"Somebody's taken very good care of this gun," he said. "If you take good care of them, they last practically forever."

"It was my great-grandmother's," Susan said. "She had it in China."

"Most family heirlooms are ugly paintings of ugly people," he said, "or umbrella stands made out of an elephant's foot. Or a moose head. I think you lucked out getting something like this. How come Randy didn't get it?"

"Grandpa left it to me," Susan said. "That sort of tore Randy up."

"I'll bet it did," Ted said, and laughed. He screwed the cleaning rod together and then screwed a wire brush in the end of it.

"Do you really want to clean that yourself? Or do you want me to?"

"I want to do it," she said. "Does that make me seem unfeminine?"

"Not at all," he said. "The first thing you do is dip the patch in the solvent. Then you run it all the way through each barrel and back out, ten times."

He demonstrated, and then let her do it. As she was working, he rummaged in the drawer end and came up with another rod. "I thought there would be two," he said, and took Doctor Hebard's shotgun apart and began to work the brush in its barrels.

He then showed her how to replace the bristle brush with a jag, a piece of metal with a hole in it to hold cleaning patches. This was run through the bores ten times too, and then the dirty patches were replaced with clean ones.

After these had been run through several times, he took the barrels from her and held them up to the light.

"Spotless," he said. "A shotgun barrel gets better with use, did you know that?"

"No," she said. "But I'm glad to hear it."

He showed her how to clean the interior of the action, and then how to wipe the whole gun with a slightly oiled rag before putting it back together and into the rack.

"I hate to shine my shoes," he said, "and if I wasn't in ROTC, I think I'd grow a beard. I'm lazy, maybe sloppy, in other words, but I never seem to mind cleaning a gun. I suppose that makes me some sort of a nut."

"I don't think so," she said. "Although I don't think I'd like you with a beard."

"If you're through in there, children," Mrs. Hebard called, "dinner's ready."

Susan winced. Ted winked at her. "After you, child," he said with a smile.

The table was elaborately set. Mrs. Hebard was putting on a show. Doctor Maroney had been to dinner countless times before, but the table had never been quite so fancy before.

Mrs. Hebard was delighted with the world in general, and the reason was quite clear. Charley Kowalski, high school dropout, veteran, scion of the junkyard Kowalski, had been neatly replaced by Ted Maroney, doctor's son and university student.

When dinner was over, they got into the Fiat and drove out to the highway.

"Where are we headed?" Susan asked. "Where's the party?" Then she remembered that her mother had asked no questions about their destination or their expected time of return.

"The country club," he said. "Where else would you expect the doctor's son to take the doctor's daughter?"

"I don't think I like that," she said. "It sounds snobbish."

"I've been thinking it over," he said, "and I decided that I like Charley so well that I don't like you going out with me just to make him jealous."

She thought about that a minute and laughed.

"What's so funny?" he asked.

"I guess it looks like that," she said. "But I didn't come tonight to make Charley jealous."

"Why, then?"

"My father laid down the law this morning that I can't go out with Charley except on every third date. You're number one, and then I get somebody else to take me out. And then . . ."

"Then you go out with Charley?"

"Then I wait for Charley to ask me," she said. "Which may be a long wait. My mother made it perfectly clear to him that he was the older man taking advantage of the young and innocent girl. The trouble is, I think he believes it."

"You're a *rara avis*," he said.

"What's that supposed to mean?"

"*Rara avis*, rare bird, a truthful female," he said. "And turn about is fair play. Would you be furious if I told you I had an ulterior motive in asking you to come to the party with me?"

"That depends on just what the motive was."

"It's going to make me sound like I've got a very flattering opinion of myself."

"Go on," she said.

"It recently occurred to me that I am thought of as an eligible bachelor," Ted said. "And, oddly enough, this isn't the unqualified delight that you might think. It's not that I don't like the interest of the ladies. I do. But the trouble is that their interest in me is based on what they think I am, rather than what I really am."

"What's the difference? I mean, between what they think you are, and what you really are?"

"All mothers . . . yours, too, I'll bet . . . take one look at me and form the unshakable opinion that I'm going to be a doctor, like Dad, and in the back of their minds is the fact that my mother's family doesn't have to worry much about money."

"You're not going to be a doctor?"

"Does that shock you?"

"I guess I'm no better than the rest," she admitted.

"I don't know what I'm going to be," he said. "But I'll tell you this, Susan. I've decided that I'm much too young to start making plans to get married the minute I finish college, or medical school. I asked you to go with me tonight for very selfish reasons."

"Such as?"

"You didn't seem too impressed with me, for one thing," he said, "and when I see my mother next weekend, she will be delighted that I 'saw' a nice girl like you."

"Well," Susan said, her ego slightly bumped. "That makes sense I guess."

"I think there must be a happy medium somewhere between staying completely away from the ladies, and having an 'understanding' thirty minutes after you start the first date."

"We're coming to that," she said.

"Huh?"

"Your parents want you to go out with me, because I'm a 'nice' girl," she said, "and my parents are pleased that you're taking me out, because you're a 'nice' boy. Right?"

"I see your point," he said.

"Friends?" she asked, and put out her hand.

"Friends," he said, shaking it. "The beauty of this understanding is that I think we can have some fun, too."

"How do you mean that?"

"You're the first girl I've met who looked like she enjoyed shooting, instead of just putting up with it because I'm a shooter."

"OK," she said. "We have a deal."

To Susan the party was a success. Randy was there, not surprisingly with Alice Gunter. Two things became immediately apparent, first that Alice clearly regarded Ted Maroney as a greater social catch than Cousin Randy, and that

Cousin Randy himself would be perfectly delighted to ingratiate himself with Ted.

Susan discovered that she wasn't above displaying a few feminine claws of her own, and that there was a degree of satisfaction in it.

As Susan was combing her hair in the ladies' room, Alice sidled up beside her and purred, "I'm so glad to see you here, Susan."

Susan was shocked, but not displeased, to hear herself purr back: "Well, there really wasn't much else doing tonight, and Ted said he didn't mind coming here just this once."

"I didn't know you were dating him," Alice blurted.

"Oh, we're old friends," Susan said.

"Just friends?" Alice said.

"What else?" Susan said, smiling just as artificially as Alice had smiled at her.

Randy, too, managed to get his two cents in, and his nose disjointed slightly. He cut in when Susan was dancing with Terry Stevens.

"I'm glad to see that you're out with Ted," he said.

"Why?" she asked.

"Well, he's a nice guy. He's a fraternity brother of mine."

"Is that so?"

"Didn't he tell you?"

"I guess he didn't think it was important," Susan said. "We don't talk much about things like that."

Susan quickly saw that simply being out with Ted made her stock rise with the other boys. Terry Stevens hovered around their table, and it wasn't hard to read on his face that he knew Ted was at the university, and not around town most of the time. It was also obvious that he was just waiting for a chance to ask Susan for a date. She wished he would, and get it over with. Going out with Terry would make it Date Number Two, and then she would be free to go out again with Charley, if and when he asked her.

Ted was magnificent. He seemed to sense the precise moment when he should reappear on the scene.

"Terry was just asking me if I'd go out with him on Friday night," Susan said. Terry looked as if he had been caught doing something wrong.

"I'll be away next weekend," Ted said, "I don't suppose there would be any harm, seeing it's Terry." The implication was that Terry was as dangerous to their romance as Randy would be, which is to say, no danger whatever.

By the time they left the country club, Susan felt just slightly smug. It was clearly established in everyone's mind that she and Ted had an 'understanding.' She felt that she had met the establishment in fair battle and won on her own terms.

When he dropped her off at her house, Ted said, "Thank you, partner. You turned what had all the makings of a royal bore of an evening into a lot of fun. I'll see you in two weeks?"

"It's a date," she said.

As she walked up the steps onto the porch, he called out, "When you see Charley, tell him hello for me, will you?"

10

In Automotive Shop on Monday afternoon, Charley seemed to be avoiding her, so she gathered her courage and walked over to where he was working on the old Chevrolet transmission.

"I saw an old friend of yours over the weekend," she said. "He said to say hello."

"Who's that?"

"Ted Maroney."

He nodded, but said nothing.

"I'm sorry about what happened at the house," she said, with an effort.

"I don't blame your mother," he said. "If I had a daughter like you . . ."

"Don't be a fool," she said.

"I'm not," he said. "Excuse me." And he walked away.

She had been put down, and there was absolutely nothing she could do about it.

Aside from a slight nod, and an even fainter smile, Charley Kowalski scarcely acknowledged her presence for the rest of the week. And not because there wasn't an opportunity.

The crankshaft came back from the machine shop, and the whole class gathered to watch as it was reinstalled, complete with new bearings, into the engine block. By the time the warning bell rang on Friday the engine was half-way reassembled.

She threw caution to the winds when she found herself alone with Charley.

"My parents said that I can go out with you every third date," she blurted. "I went out with Ted last Saturday, and I'm going out with Terry Stevens tonight."

He looked at her for a moment, then carefully looked at his hands as he wiped the grease off them with a rag.

"Have a good time with Terry," he said.

"You make me as mad as my mother does," she said, and stormed out of the shop.

Terry Stevens showed up on time that night, driving his father's car. She was tempted to plead a headache to get out of going with him, but her sense of fair play kept her from doing it.

Her mother was very cordial to Terry, if not quite as cordial as she had been to Ted. Susan wondered if this was because her mother had known Ted longer and was

134

friendly with his parents, or whether the nasty suspicion that her mother was just like the other mothers Ted had talked about was true.

An hour after they left, they were back, and Terry refused Mrs. Hebard's invitation to come in for a cup of coffee and a piece of cake.

"I gather you and Terry didn't hit it off?" her father asked.

"That's something of an understatement," Susan said.

"Well, Ted'll be back next week," her mother said.

"I think I'll go to bed," Susan said. "I have a headache." She really had one, after what had happened with Terry.

"If you feel better by tomorrow afternoon," Doctor Hebard called after her, "we could go bust some birds."

"It's a date," she said.

When he picked her up, and they were on the way to the skeet range, Susan decided to tell him about it.

"I found out that mother was right about reputations," she said.

"How's that?"

"Terry thought I had one," she said.

"Stop beating around the bush," her father said.

"He started to get fresh before the coming attractions were over," she said. "And when I gave him the speech about not being that kind of girl, he made it perfectly plain that if I went out with Charley, and then with Ted, I certainly must be that kind of girl."

"I'm sorry," her father said. "I don't know what help I can be."

"Oh, I handled him all right," she said. "I told him if he didn't stop, I'd make him wish he had."

"I'm almost afraid to ask, but you've got my curiosity up. What did you do?"

"I turned on his headlights and blew his horn. They threw us out."

Her father smiled. "Well, I'm sure that was effective in turning him off, but I don't know what good it did your reputation."

"I thought virtue was supposed to be its own reward," she said.

"It is," he said. "Do you want me to say something to Terry's parents?"

"I can handle him," Susan said. "I guess I just wanted you to know what happened when I went out with a 'nice' boy."

"I gather that Ted was a gentleman," he said.

"He's a good guy," Susan said. "A very good guy."

"I think you'll find that there are more good guys than bad guys," her father said. "It's just that the bad guys make themselves known more often."

"I told Charley what you said about every third date," she said.

"And?"

"I think Mother can relax," Susan said. "She and Charley are apparently in agreement that he's much too old for me."

"Well, Ted's not a bad consolation prize, as consolation prizes go," her father said. "If you're interested in older men, Ted's older than you are."

"Mother had no right to do what she did," Susan said, not amused.

"So long as she thought she was acting in your best interest, she did," Doctor Hebard said. "Relax, Susan. You've got all the time in the world."

"I think I'll break twenty-five straight today," she said.

"Modesty?"

"I'm so mad, I feel like breaking something."

She broke fifteen targets, then seventeen, and on the third round, twelve.

When they got home, Mrs. Hebard said that Terry had called and would call back.

After what had happened, Susan was surprised to find that he had the gall to actually ask her to go to the drive-in with him again.

"You've got your nerve, I'll say that for you," she said.

"Well, how about it?"

"I wouldn't go to the drive-in with you if you were the last male alive," she said. "Is that clear enough?"

"Suit yourself, sweetheart," he said, snorted and hung up.

"Are you going out with Terry again, dear?" her mother asked when she walked into the living room.

"No, I'm not," she said.

"Didn't he ask you?"

"I told him I was busy," Susan said.

"Oh, now you've hurt his feelings," Mrs. Hebard said. "I sort of let him know that so far as I knew, you didn't have any plans for the evening."

Susan tried to think of something to say. For a long time nothing came into her mind. Finally she said, "I'm going to clean my shotgun tonight."

Her mother looked at her as if she thought Susan was out of her mind.

In shop on Monday the heads of the engine were bolted back in place and torqued to the proper tension. Charley did the work as Mr. Fogarty explained to the class what was being done. Charley seemed uneasy when he looked at Susan, as if he wanted to say something. Whatever it was, he never got around to saying it on Monday.

But on Tuesday, when she walked into shop, he was standing by the door waiting for her.

"What you said about your parents saying it would be all right, every third date?" Charley asked.

"What about it?"

"Movies, Friday?" he asked.

"It's a date," she said.

"Good," he said, and for the first time in two weeks he smiled. That day they reinstalled the water pump and the generator.

On Wednesday, Susan was called to the principal's office. Mrs. Rogers, her guidance counselor, was there, as well as Mr. Fogarty, and the principal.

"Come on in, Susan, and close the door," said Mr. Toland, the principal.

When she was called from class to the school office Susan was always afraid that something very bad had happened, an accident or a death. Now she sensed immediately that nothing like that had happened, but at the same time she also sensed that something she wouldn't like was about to happen.

"How are you today?" Mr. Toland asked.

"Very well, thank you."

"Please sit down, Susan," he said. "We have something of a problem to solve, a problem which concerns you, and we want to talk to you about it."

"Yes, sir," she said.

"I'm afraid we made a mistake, Susan," Mr. Toland said. "All of us. Mr. Fogarty, Mrs. Rogers, and me. And you, too, really, in the final analysis."

"I don't understand you, I'm afraid," Susan said. "What kind of a mistake?"

"When all the factors are taken into consideration . . . ," Mr. Toland said, and Susan had the sudden and somewhat disrespectful thought that Mr. Toland was simply fascinated with big words. He sounded like a government publication. "It really isn't feasible for you to take automotive shop."

"Why not? If I can ask?"

"Certainly, you can ask. The purpose of this conference is to lay everything out on the table so that we can examine the problem objectively from several points of view."

"Well, then, why not?"

"The thing is, Susan," said Mr. Toland, exactly like he was presenting this astonishing fact for the first time, "you are a girl."

With an effort, she kept herself from saying that she knew she was a girl.

Mr. Toland laughed artificially. "You know there really aren't many girl mechanics."

"I suppose not."

"On the other hand, there are a great many boys who are interested in becoming mechanics, or at least, in learning something about how an automobile functions."

"That's why I enrolled in the class," Susan said. "To learn something about cars. I really hadn't planned on becoming a mechanic."

Neither Mr. Toland or Mr. Fogarty seemed to detect anything wrong with this reply, but from the look on Mrs. Rogers' face Susan knew that she had heard the sarcasm and didn't like it at all.

"I'm sure you didn't," Mr. Toland said. "But the point is, you are in the class and, as I said before, you are a girl."

"Yes, sir," Susan replied.

"There are some places, I'm afraid, that are . . . inappropriate . . . for girls."

Like the boys' locker room, Susan thought, but she didn't say anything.

"And we think one of these places is Mr. Fogarty's automotive shop."

"I'm afraid that something has happened," Mr. Toland said. "A very regrettable incident."

"Something I did?" Susan asked, completely confused.

"Not something you did," Mr. Toland replied, "but, in the final analysis, I think we must all come to the conclusion that you were in fact at least partially responsible."

"What happened? Are you going to tell me?"

"Charley Kowalski wiped up the boys' locker room with Terry Stevens," Mr. Fogarty said, getting right to the point.

"He did? Why?"

"He won't say," Mr. Fogarty said.

"If you don't mind, Mr. Fogarty," Mr. Toland said, sharply. "I will conduct our little conference."

"Sorry," Mr. Fogarty said. He didn't sound very sorry.

"Unfortunately," Mr. Toland said, "Mr. Fogarty's figure of speech is apt, rather painfully apt. Specifically, the Kowalski boy allegedly forced the Stevens' boy's face and upper body into the basin at the entrance to the showers. The basin which contains the antibacterial substance designed to reduce or eliminate the danger of athlete's foot."

"That green rubber tray affair, Susan," Mrs. Rogers said. "There's one in the girls' locker room, too."

"I know what you mean," Susan said. "Charley rubbed Terry's face in it?"

"So it is alleged," Mr. Toland said.

"Why? And what has this got to do with me?"

"For reasons I don't quite understand, both Stevens and

Kowalski are reluctant, or more precisely, refuse to discuss the matter. As a matter of fact, we didn't quite know what was wrong with the Stevens boy until your father identified the substance on his face and chest."

"My father?"

"Mr. Lupinsky, the assistant physical education instructor, was the first to notice that something was wrong with the Stevens boy. Terry's eyes were watering, apparently, and Mr. Lupinsky sent him to the school nurse. The school nurse sent him to the hospital. Your father was on emergency duty, and washed out his eyes. We learned from him that the irritant was foot-bath bactericide. We proceeded in our investigation of the matter from that point."

"Oh," Susan said.

"Now, we don't know for sure, Susan," Mr. Fogarty said, apparently deciding to ignore Mr. Toland, "but what it looks like is that Charley and Terry had a fight, and the fight was over you. Neither of them will say anything about it. Terry says he slipped, but we heard another story, too."

"Quite," Mr. Toland said.

"Why were they fighting about me?"

"It seems that Terry said something about you to which Kowalski took exception," Mr. Toland said.

"Oh," Susan said. She suddenly knew with a horrible feeling what Terry probably said. "But I still don't understand what this has got to do with me in Mr. Fogarty's class."

"Through no fault of your own," Mr. Toland said, "I'm afraid that you're a disruptive influence."

"No one suggests that you're in any way at fault," Mrs. Rogers said. "Men have been fighting over women for a long time. The point is that we must do what we can to prevent further incidents like this."

"We've decided that you should drop out of the automotive class, Susan," Mr. Toland said. "For the general good of all concerned."

"That makes it look like I'm responsible for what Charley did to Terry," Susan said, "as if I set it up."

"No one has made such a suggestion," Mr. Toland said.

"That's what it will look like," Susan said.

Mr. Toland gave her a look that made it quite clear he didn't like her attitude.

"I have discussed the matter with your father," he said. "And he fully agrees with my suggestion that you drop out of the class."

"I see," Susan said. "Then there's not much use in discussing it, is there?"

"I had hoped that you would understand our position," Mr. Toland said. "Especially in view of the fact that we have decided not to institute disciplinary action against Kowalski."

"If Charley clobbered Stevens, Terry had it coming to him," Susan said. "Charley's not a bully."

"Mr. Fogarty made that point," Mr. Toland said, "but the point is that serious damage could have been done to the

Stevens boy, and we simply can't permit fighting in school, no matter what the alleged provocation."

"It looks as if I'm being . . . tossed out . . . of the automotive shop class."

"Not necessarily," Mrs. Rogers said. "It can be explained just as easily as a simple matter of you realizing that the automotive shop is no place for a girl."

"And it really isn't, Susan," Mr. Fogarty said.

"On that point, we are all agreed. And so, I might add, is Doctor Hebard."

She shrugged. There was obviously nothing she could say.

"Now you have your option of secretarial science or a study hall, Susan," Mrs. Rogers said. "Which would you prefer?"

"Study hall, I guess," Susan said. "I already know how to type."

"Very well. Just go to study hall instead of to automotive shop this afternoon," Mrs. Rogers said.

"That will be all, Susan," Mr. Toland said. "Thank you for coming by."

Susan looked at Mr. Fogarty. He met her eyes and shrugged his shoulders. She knew then that Mr. Fogarty believed that Charley had had good provocation, and that he hadn't been anxious to get her out of the class. The decision to have her leave the class had been unanimous only because Mr. Toland was the principal.

Alice Gunter was standing in the corridor outside the study hall when Susan went there.

"Well, I hope you've learned your lesson," she said. "For your sake I just hope that Ted doesn't hear about all this."

"About all what, Alice?" Susan asked.

"I just don't understand you any more," Alice said. "You've changed so much that I simply don't understand you."

"How would you like to have your face dunked in the footbath, Alice?" Susan said, and then walked into the study hall to present her Change of Curriculum card to the teacher in charge.

Toward the end of the period she went to the pencil sharpener and looked out the window in time to see the old convertible being towed away by a wrecker from the Cadillac garage.

She spent the rest of the period stewing over what was happening to her car.

After school, she went to her father's office. He wasn't there but she found him at the hospital. He didn't seem surprised to see her.

"You don't look like a *femme fatale*," he said with a smile.

"Very funny," she said.

"What can I do for you," Doctor Hebard asked.

"Where did they take my car?"

"You found out about that, did you? Don't get concerned. I had the Cadillac people take it down there to finish putting it back together. It won't take them long, and the price wasn't nearly as stiff as I thought it would be. You'll have the car in a week with a paint job thrown in."

"Oh," she said.

"How about 'thank you'?" her father asked.

"I'm sorry," she said. "Thank you."

"You're welcome," he said. "Is that all you had on your mind?"

"Well, you know what else happened," she said.

"I put a call in to Terry's father," he said. "I haven't reached him yet, but I will."

"What for?"

"To tell him the next time that kid of his runs off at the mouth about my daughter *I'll* throw him in the footbath."

"I wish you'd stay out of it," she said.

"I don't see how I can stay out of it," he said.

"Please just let it go, will you?" she asked. "Let it die out."

"That's the trouble with these things, Susan. Once they start they just won't die."

"Does Mother know?"

"I didn't tell her, but I will if she asks. I have the feeling there will be a half a dozen 'friends' on the telephone by suppertime to offer their sympathy."

"I've got a date with Charley Friday night," Susan said. "What about that?"

He looked at her for a moment. "I keep my bargains," he said. "You know that."

II

Her mother was tight-lipped and cold when Susan got home from the hospital. Without being told, Susan knew that her father had called while she was en route and "discussed" the issue with her mother. Susan knew that her father's amiability was often mistaken for softness by other people. But she had long ago learned that there was no question in her mother's mind about who ran the family. He didn't often give orders or insist on anything, but when he had made up his mind to permit something or to do something that was the way it happened.

He had obviously called and told Mrs. Hebard that Susan was going out with Charley, and with his permission.

It turned out to be unnecessary. Susan was dressed and waiting for Charley at half past six. By half past seven it was obvious that Charley wasn't going to show up.

At quarter to eight the telephone rang. The whole family

was in the library, watching a situation comedy Susan thought was an incredibly bad television program.

Susan thought that the caller might be Charley, and this time she had enough presence of mind to remember that she had sort of thrown herself at him, and she decided she wouldn't give him the satisfaction of answering the telephone on the second ring. Or at all.

Mrs. Hebard was similarly unwilling to answer the phone. Doctor Hebard finally got up, walked to the table, and picked up the phone.

"Just a moment," he said, and made a gesture with his hand, indicating that the call was for Susan.

"I'll take it in the kitchen," she said, and walked very slowly to the kitchen.

"Hello," she said, and at that moment she heard a click telling her that her father had hung up.

"What's new, Deadeye?" Ted Maroney asked.

"Oh," she said. "It's you."

"I'm deeply touched by your wild enthusiasm," he said. "Who did you expect?"

"To tell you the truth, I've been stood up," she said. "I sort of thought maybe he'd call and offer some flimsy excuse."

"I specialize in consoling stood-up females," he said. "I just got in, Dad's at the hospital, and the prospect of eating here alone isn't very thrilling. Can I buy you a meal?"

"I've had dinner, thanks," she said. "Come on over here, if you'd like. I'll fix you a sandwich or something."

"Thanks but no thanks," he said. "I'm determined to have a meal. You can watch me eat, if you want. Doesn't bother me at all to have people watch me eat."

"I'll let you buy me a fancy dessert," she said.

"I'll be right over," he said, and hung up without saying good-bye. She went back in the living room. Her mother's curiosity was evident; Doctor Hebard hadn't volunteered the identity of the caller, and his wife hadn't been willing to ask.

"That was Ted," Susan said. "He's going to buy me a dessert."

"How nice," Mrs. Hebard said. Her relief was as evident as her curiosity had been.

In ten minutes, Susan heard Ted's Fiat, which sounded like a lazy hornet, come up the road, and then heard his footsteps on the porch.

When she let him in, she was suddenly very much aware that he was a very attractive young man. He was wearing a shirt and tie and a very elegant sports coat. He looked like an advertisement, she thought.

"It couldn't have been a very important date you missed," he said by way of greeting. "You look neither heartbroken nor furious."

"I'm a stoic," she said. "Remember, 'laugh and the world laughs with you; cry and you cry alone.' "

"Oh, goody," he said. "I always wanted to go out with a girl who was intellectual and spoke profundities."

"It would improve your mind," Susan countered.

"Have you got any hot plans for next weekend?" he asked.

"No," she said. "What's on your mind?"

He gestured for her to follow him. He went into the library.

"Mrs. Hebard," he said, "would you trust your daughter to the care of my mother?"

"Whatever are you talking about?"

"Well, there's a dinner dance next weekend at the fraternity, and I've been given the word that I will be there."

"And you want Susan to go, and stay with your mother?" Mrs. Hebard said.

"Uh-huh."

"Why, certainly, Ted," Mrs. Hebard said, "I'm sure she'd have a lovely time."

"The party is going to be a royal bore, I'm afraid," Ted said, "but there is some compensation. Hunting season opens on Saturday morning, and I have a farmer friend who swears his fields are crawling with pheasant."

"Oh," Mrs. Hebard said, making it quite plain that she was far more enthusiastic about the dance than the hunting. "Susan's never been hunting."

"It's about time," Ted said.

"Nobody's asked me yet," Susan said.

"Well, what about it?" Ted said. "Do you want to go?"

"Why not?" Susan said. "Yes, thank you. I accept."

"If Doctor Hebard thinks it's all right," Mrs. Hebard said formally.

"I think it would be an interesting experience for Susan,"

Doctor Hebard said. "Both the dance and the hunting. How's she going to get over there, Ted? Have you thought about that?"

"That poses something of a problem," he said. "It's a two-hour drive. Three hours on the bus. Would it be all right with you if she went on the bus? I'll bring her home Saturday evening."

"There's really no reason why she couldn't drive herself over there," Doctor Hebard said. "And drive herself home, too."

"I don't know," Mrs. Hebard said.

"It's a four-lane highway, and she'd be traveling in the daytime," Doctor Hebard said. "If we're going to throw her out of the nest, let's give her a good toss."

"I don't think I like your choice of words," Mrs. Hebard said.

"I don't want to ride the bus," Susan said.

"Oh, I know about this dance," Mrs. Hebard said, suddenly remembering something. "Aunt Marge told me about it. Randy's taking Alice Gunter."

"Until just now," Susan said, "I was looking forward to it."

"Perhaps you and Alice could go together," Mrs. Hebard said.

"If I have to go with Alice, I'm not going," Susan said.

Mrs. Hebard didn't want the family linen washed in front of Ted.

"We'll work something out, Ted," she said. "And I'll call you mother and give her the details."

"Thank you," Ted said. "Come on, Deadeye, you can watch me eat."

She did just that. Ted drove to the Old Hungarian restaurant and consumed a huge meal, including chicken paprika. He introduced Susan to a Hungarian dish whose name she immediately forgot, but it consisted of strawberries rolled up in sweet pancakes. The dessert was almost a meal in itself.

Then he drove her back to the farm, and announced, "I'll pick you up tomorrow at nine."

"What happens then?"

"We spend the morning at the skeet range," he said. "I intend to dazzle my friends with your marksmanship as well as your charm and beauty."

"OK," she said, pleased. As she watched him drive away, she thought he really was a nice guy and that it was a shame, almost sad, that that's all he was, a nice guy, something like a brother.

Doctor Hebard invited himself along in the morning, and Susan understood what his motives were. He wanted to be sure that she knew enough about shooting so she'd be safe when hunting with Ted. She shot well and in one round broke eighteen of the twenty-five targets.

Doctor Maroney appeared at the range before they left, and Susan was not blind to the fact that as far as the two fathers were concerned, she and Ted made a very nice couple.

They all went to a hamburger stand for lunch, and then Ted left, saying that he was expected at his mother's for dinner, and that he would see her at his mother's sometime on the afternoon of the following Friday.

At breakfast on Wednesday, Doctor Hebard told Susan that he was taking her shopping. She didn't know why.

"What kind of shopping?"

"For your first university weekend," he said. "You're going away, remember?"

"She has that black velvet dress, which is perfectly all right," Mrs. Hebard said.

"She'll look kind of silly hunting pheasant in a black velvet dress," Doctor Hebard said.

"I'd forgotten about that. What am I supposed to wear?"

"What your Wise Old Dad is going to buy for you after school today," he said.

"I wish she wasn't going hunting," Mrs. Hebard said. "It just doesn't seem . . . appropriate."

"She's been asked, she's accepted, and she's going," Doctor Hebard said.

Alice Gunter and her mother came into Gregory's Department Store as Susan was trying on a pair of leather hunting boots.

"What in the world are you doing?" Alice asked.

"I'm going hunting over the weekend," Susan said. "These are hunting boots."

"So I see," Alice said. "Well, each to his own, I suppose. I'm going over to the university this weekend. With Randy. To a fraternity dance."

"Have a good time," Susan said.

Mrs. Gunter looked uneasy at the rather obvious hostility between the girls, but, like Doctor Hebard, she seemed to understand that they were a little too old to be shaken by the shoulder and told to make up.

When Susan and her father returned to the farm, she saw the old Cadillac parked in front of the house. Mrs. Hebard was also waiting, and she did not seem very happy.

"Well, they delivered it when they said they would, didn't they?" Doctor Hebard said.

"Mr. Lewison himself brought it out," Mrs. Hebard said. Mr. Lewison was the proprietor of the Cadillac agency. "I guess he was afraid to send someone else with it."

She gestured with a large yellow sheet of paper before handing it to her husband. It was obviously the bill. Doctor Hebard took it, looked at it, and said, "Ouch!"

"You could almost have bought a new one for that kind of money," Mrs. Hebard said. "It's a . . . disgrace. It's just wasteful."

"I don't think so," Doctor Hebard said. "I think it'll be worth it in the long run."

He draped his arm around Susan's shoulder. "It looks good, doesn't it, honey? Let's see if it runs."

"For that kind of money," Mrs. Hebard said, not very pleasantly, "it should fly."

"Thank you, Daddy," Susan said.

"Come on, Phyllis," Doctor Hebard said. "Be a sport. Go for a ride with us."

"I don't . . ." she said, and then: "Well, I might as well, I suppose."

"I'll get in the back, make believe I'm the prince of some unpronounceable Arab country, and wave at the people," Doctor Hebard said.

"You're not going to put the top down," Mrs. Hebard protested.

"There's no sense in having a convertible if you leave the roof up," he said.

Susan started the engine and then unfastened the top. She pulled on the top control and it folded neatly into the body.

"I feel ridiculous," Mrs. Hebard said. "This thing belongs in a museum."

"Just smile and wave at the people," Doctor Hebard said, "to show them we in the palace have their best interests at heart."

Mrs. Hebard had to give in. "You're a nut," she said. "The two of you are both nuts." But she laughed.

They took a five mile drive, stopping halfway to put the top up. Convertible or not, it was just too late in the year to ride around with it down.

"Well, I'm willing to admit that it rides very well," Mrs. Hebard said, "but I hate to think what the gasoline bills are going to be like."

"That's what I've always liked about you," Doctor Hebard said. "You always find the silver lining in the dark cloud."

Mrs. Hebard had another thought. "You aren't proposing that she drive this to the university?"

"I certainly am," Doctor Hebard said so quickly that Susan didn't really have time to become concerned.

"I'll worry all the time she's on the road," Mrs. Hebard said.

"You'd be worried even if I sent her in an ambulance with a police escort," Doctor Hebard said. "We'll both be worried, I suppose."

"Well, at least she'll be with Ted. And his mother, of course," Mrs. Hebard said, consoling herself.

Susan took a good deal of pleasure in driving the car alone for the first time when she drove to school the next day. During the last period she looked out the window again and saw that Charley Kowalski was examining the car in some detail. But by the time she got down to it when the period was over, he was gone. She didn't see him on Friday, either.

The drive to Ted's mother's house was uneventful. Because the engine had to be broken in, she couldn't go faster than fifty miles. Her father had also told her that she shouldn't maintain that speed, but should go slower and then up to fifty and then slower again instead.

She'd almost arrived when a car passed her doing at least seventy-five. She glowered at it, and then at the same moment saw the driver put on his brakes and Alice's face in the window. It was Alice and Randy.

Susan waved gaily at them, and after a moment, Randy stepped on the gas again and the car moved far ahead of her and then out of sight.

She found Ted's mother's house without much trouble, and Mrs. Maroney seemed very pleased to see her. It wasn't hard to figure out what she was thinking. Ted had found a nice girl. This wasn't as flattering as it might have been, because no matter how good a guy Ted was, she wasn't his girl. She wondered if that made her whole trip over here a deception somehow, or dishonest.

Ted arrived fifteen minutes after she did, and was obviously pleased to see her.

"Hey, Deadeye," he said. "Remember to bring your gun?"

"A very gentlemanly speech to a young lady, I must say. 'Hey, Deadeye, did you bring your gun?' " Mrs. Maroney said.

"It's what's known as the generation gap," Ted said. "I saw the car. Magnificent. I don't suppose you'd want to drive me to the party in it?"

"I should say not," Mrs. Maroney said. "She's your guest, and you'll drive her in your car."

It didn't seem worth making an issue over, so they went to the party in Ted's car, with the roof up.

Susan had a good time at the party. She was a little uneasy at first, because she realized high school seniors were not normally invited to parties like this.

Alice didn't seem very surprised to see her and decided to be cordial. She spoke first, on the dance floor, making some inane remark about how nice Susan looked, and minutes later, when Susan was sitting alone with Ted at the table, Alice and Randy came over and sat down.

"We passed you on the highway, didn't we?" Alice asked.

"As if I was standing still," Susan said.

"I hear that you had to have the Cadillac people put Grandpa's car back together," Randy said.

"Is that the car you were going to get for the fraternity?" Ted asked. Susan saw that he'd just connected the two facts.

"She wouldn't sell it," Randy said, uncomfortably.

"The way you told it, it was yours," Ted said.

"It should have been," Randy said.

"I thought you said that Charley Kowalski was rebuilding it for you, Susan?" Ted asked.

"That's a very delicate subject," Alice said.

"How come?" Ted asked.

"I really don't think we should talk about it," Alice said, primly. "It's done and over with."

Ted looked at Susan with a question in his eyes.

"I was a disruptive influence in the automotive shop," Susan said. "They threw me and the car out."

"I probably shouldn't say this," Alice said. "But, really, it is a little thrilling. Having boys fight over you, I mean."

"Really?" Ted said, with delight on his face. "I'm fascinated. Who fought?"

"Terry Stevens and a mechanic named Kowalski," Randy said. "Or so I hear."

"Charley Kowalski?" Ted asked.

"His family owns the junkyard," Alice volunteered in much the same tone of voice she would have used to announce that Charley was a leper.

"I think Alice is right," Randy announced. "The less said

158

about the matter, the better. Anyway, it's all over. I settled Mr. Kowalski's hash."

"I beg your pardon?" Susan asked.

"You heard me," Randy said.

"We both heard you," Ted said, "but we don't understand you."

"Well, if you insist. I told him to stay away from you."

"You did what?" Susan asked, rage building up inside her.

"I told him that if he knew what was good for him, he'd stay away from you."

"Or you would do something about it?" Ted asked sarcastically.

"After all, Susan is my cousin," Randy said, a good deal louder than necessary. "I have an obligation to her."

Ted laughed.

"What's so funny?"

"Randy threatening Charley Kowalski is about like a mosquito picking a fight with an elephant," Ted said. "Did he laugh in your face?"

"He knew I meant business," Randy said.

"You keep your two cents out of my business in the future, Randy, or you will have a fight on your hands," Susan said.

Ted got to his feet. He was laughing. "I suppose I'd better dance with you," he said, "before you do take a swing at Randy."

They danced a couple of minutes before Ted spoke.

"What was the fight all about?" he asked.

"Terry Stevens made a pass at me," Susan said. "When I turned him down, he apparently told the story the other way. Charley rubbed his face in the athlete's foot basin in the boys' locker room."

Ted laughed out loud. "Marvelous," he said. "Good for Charley."

People were looking at them, and Susan was embarrassed.

"You're sort of stuck on Charley, aren't you?" Ted asked softly.

"I guess," Susan said after a moment's thought. "But it's the original lost cause."

"How come? Is he blind?"

"He and my mother have decided that he's bad for me," Susan said.

"As well as Brother Randy, I gather," Ted said.

"Cousin Randy," she corrected automatically.

"Your cousin, my fraternity brother," he said. "Friends to the end. One for all and all for one, with other assorted adolescent mumbo-jumbo."

"Why do you put up with it, if you don't like it?"

"It's a lot easier not to buck the system—which means Mother—by being antisocial," Ted said. "Besides, the food's not bad here."

She chuckled, but the business with Randy had effectively ruined the evening and they both knew it. They were among the first to leave the party.

12

Susan awoke with a start. It was quite dark in the room, and for a moment she had no idea where she was.

"Hey, Deadeye," Ted's voice called from behind the door. "You awake?"

"I'm awake," she said. "I'll be right out."

She put on her hunting clothes and went out of the room with her shotgun and downstairs into the kitchen.

Mrs. Maroney was at the stove wearing a dressing gown.

"Your mother must think I'm terrible," she said, "letting Ted do this to you."

"Do what to me?"

"Waking you up to go hunting in the middle of the night after a party."

"I want to go," Susan said. "And he brought me home early."

"Then you must have gone back to the party?" Mrs.

Maroney said. "I heard the phone ring. And then later about three, I heard the door open."

"I'm the sergeant-at-arms," Ted said. "And one of my beloved brothers got drunk, and I had to put him to bed and then take his date home."

"Oh, Ted. I thought they had a rule about liquor at parties."

"Some people have to prove they're men," he said. "By either threatening to get violent, or getting drunk." He looked at Susan significantly, and she knew the identity of the drunk. "But no lasting harm was done, I suppose."

"Gives Susan a fine impression of your fraternity, though, doesn't it?" Mrs. Maroney asked.

"He wasn't drunk when we were there," Ted said.

"Well, I'm sorry, Susan," Mrs. Maroney said.

There was a sudden white glow of headlights in the driveway, the sound of a car door slamming, then a knock on the kitchen door. Ted pulled it open and two young men in hunting clothes came in. They had been at the party the night before, but Susan couldn't remember their names.

"Good morning, Mrs. Maroney," they said, almost in unison, and then one said, "So she really is going hunting," and the other said, "Who owns that gorgeous machine in the driveway?"

"She really is going hunting, and she owns that gorgeous machine," Ted said.

"Would you like something to eat?" Mrs. Maroney said.

"No, thanks, we stopped at a diner," the taller of the two said.

"Well, you'll just have to wait until Susan has something. I'm opposed to sending her out hunting in the middle of the night, and I refuse to send her out without something to eat."

After they had eaten and left the house, the newcomers paused to look again at the old Cadillac.

"Why don't we take it?" Susan asked.

That the boys wanted to was evident. But it was equally evident that their male pride was involved; the man is supposed to provide the wheels. A reason would have to be found.

"It would save taking both cars," one of them finally said, gesturing to a Volkswagen parked in the drive. "Of course, we could take the Bug, but it would be crowded."

"You wouldn't mind, Susan? We'll buy the gas."

"Like he said," Susan said, "it would save taking two cars, and it would be crowded in the Volkswagen."

"I wouldn't mind the crowding, if you'd ride in the back with me," the taller of the two said.

"Get your guns, Romeo," Ted said, "and put them in the back where you'll sit."

"Since I don't know where we're going, you'd better tell me," Susan said.

They drove through town and then onto a secondary highway in the country.

"How are things at the frat house?" Ted asked abruptly.

"When we left, he was in the john again, urping," the taller one said with some disgust. "Serves him right."

"There's more, Ted," the other one said. "I don't think

the cops know about it, but the life of the party ran into the porch."

"Much damage?"

"Not to the porch, but his car has a lov-er-ley crease across the fender. Got the headlight, and part of the grill, too."

"What about the girl?"

"My girl took her to the guest house," the taller one said. "And I don't think she liked it very much. The girl friend is an urper, too."

"Where'd he get the booze?"

"I guess he brought it with him," the taller one said. "He's a three-star moron."

"He's Susan's cousin."

"Well, that's what's known as jamming your foot in your mouth. Sorry, Susan, I didn't know."

"You're wrong," Susan said. "He's a four-star moron, maybe even five."

"I found out something else about him," Ted said. "Remember when he ran off at the mouth about the old junk he was going to get us?"

"You mean to use in parades? What about it?"

"You're riding in it," Ted said.

"You're kidding."

"No. Fortunately, Deadeye here beat him out of it."

"Good for you, Deadeye," the taller one said, "Cutting this thing up would be like painting a mustache on the Mona Lisa."

"I think I like you," said Susan. "You are obviously a man of taste and discernment."

It was daylight when they pulled up at a farm house, but there were still lights in the first floor windows. As the car pulled up, two men in hunting clothes came out of the house. As she got closer, Susan saw that it was a father-son combination.

The father didn't seem overjoyed to see her, although he was polite.

"We might as well start from the house," he said. "And work through the cornfields." He turned to Susan. "Do you plan to walk along, young lady?"

"She plans to hunt," Ted said. "That's why I brought her."

"Has she got a gun?"

"Uh-huh."

"Can she use it?"

"Very well, as a matter of fact."

"We'll see," he said. He might as well have said, "I'll believe it when I see it."

Susan was ill at ease as they made preparations to start. A very large black dog appeared from nowhere and nudged her with his nose. After a moment she realized it was a Labrador retriever. She squatted down and rubbed his ears.

"He's not used to lady hunters," the father said.

The son and the taller of the two boys got in a jeep and drove away. They would "back up" the hunt, Ted told Susan. The rest of them would walk through the cornfield in search of the pheasants.

"No hens," the father said. "Do you know the difference?"

She thought a moment and realized that she did know the difference. The female pheasant wasn't nearly as colorful as the male.

"Yes, I do," she said.

"OK, let's go," the father said. He took up a position on one side of Susan. Ted and the other boy spread out on the other side.

The father loaded his gun and then Susan loaded hers. They started to walk through the field.

At this point, Susan began to entertain very serious doubts about the wisdom of being here. There were a number of things that could go wrong. For one thing, she wasn't at all sure that she could shoot at a bird if they found one. It was also highly questionable if she would hit it when she shot at it. In either case, Ted would be embarrassed because of her, and she didn't want that to happen.

They walked slowly. The walking was rough. The corn was tall and it slapped against Susan's body and her face until she learned to use the shotgun as sort of a stick. Once she almost fell over a clod of earth and it seemed to be just one more splendid opportunity to make a fool of herself and of Ted.

When the first cock pheasant rose in front of her, it came as a complete shock. One moment there was nothing; the next second there was a loud flutter of wings and a bird headed for the sky.

Later she didn't even remember putting the gun to her

shoulder, nor the sound of it firing, nor its slap against her shoulder. What she did remember was the bird suddenly exploding in a cloud of feathers and then falling straight down.

She was startled by a rustling sound behind her, something thrashing through the rows of corn. The Labrador plunged purposefully past her.

"That's the way," a male voice said. "That was a clean kill."

She didn't like the sound of that.

And then she saw the dog trotting down the row toward her, his big tail swinging from side to side, and holding the bird in his mouth. He came to her and sat down. Susan didn't have the faintest idea of what was supposed to happen now.

"Good boy," she said to the dog, mainly because he seemed to be looking for approval.

The dog dropped the bird at her feet.

The father appeared at Susan's side. "Hey, stupid," he said with great affection, "just because the women feed you all year doesn't mean you're not my dog."

The dog wagged his tail.

The father picked up the bird and looked at it. "Nice bird," he said, and handed it to Susan. There was nothing to do but take it. She remembered that her new coat had a rubber pouch in the rear. That was obviously where the bird was supposed to go. The father suddenly tugged at the bird, took it from her, and dropped it in the back of her jacket.

"I guess he likes you," the father said. "A dog is supposed to be a pretty good judge of character."

Susan felt as if she had just been given a medal. The father disappeared through the corn rows again, and then called out. "OK, let's move the line."

Three more times before they had walked through the field, a shotgun barked, and once there was the warning shout "Hen!" Susan didn't see another bird, and she was surprised to find when they came out on the road that, despite the three shots, only one other pheasant had been killed.

The birds were put in a box on the back of the Jeep. The hunters piled in, Susan riding in front in deference to the fair sex. They drove to the next field and repeated the hunting process.

This time, when a cock rose in front of Susan, she fired her first barrel and missed. But she fired again and hit it with the second barrel. When the retriever brought her the bird she wasn't so squeamish about taking it from him and putting it in her jacket.

Ten minutes later, as they approached the end of the field, a third bird rose suddenly in front of her and she dropped it with the first shot.

There were nine birds in the box after the second field. Susan was excited and happy, but she was also just about worn out.

"Well, that's it for you and George," the father said. "You might as well put up your gun. Can you drive a Jeep?"

Susan wondered what she had done wrong.

"I'm through? I just got started."

"The law is three a day, and six in possession," the father said. "And I'm one of those oddballs who follows the spirit of the law. People shoot their own birds."

"I didn't know about the limit," Susan said, somewhat shamefacedly.

"Now you do," he said, and then he smiled. "They wrote the law for people like you who get three birds with four shells."

"That was just luck," she said.

"It wasn't all luck," he said. He repeated the question: "Can you drive a Jeep?"

"I think so," she said. "I never have, but I know how to shift."

"OK," he said. "Get in, and I'll show you where to go."

Fatigue stole over her as she waited for the others to hunt the field. She didn't have to take off her boots to know she had blisters on the balls of her feet and on her legs where the upper portions of the boots had rubbed against them. Her leg muscles also hurt, from the unaccustomed exercise.

The others had their limit by a quarter to eleven. Susan drove the Jeep back to the farm house.

"Pull up in back," the father said. "I asked my wife to get the paraffin hot for us."

A woman, obviously their host's wife, was standing beside a stainless steel cauldron that seemed to be sitting on an electric hot plate.

Her eyebrows went up when she saw Susan.

"This is a fraternity brother, Ted?" she asked.

"This is Susan Hebard, Mrs. Carlsen," Ted said.

"And you voluntarily associate with these hoodlums, dear?" Mrs. Carlsen asked.

"She got three birds with four shells, Mother," the father said.

"Did you get your limit?" Mrs. Carlsen asked.

Mr. Carlsen nodded.

"Well, you've got your work cut out for you, then," Mrs. Carlsen said. "You can help me, dear, if you'd like, while they pluck and clean the birds."

"Yes, ma'am," Susan said, and followed her into the house. Her feet and legs felt heavy. From the smell in the kitchen, they were obviously about to be fed, and Susan thought that right now the feminine role of serving food was vastly more desirable than having to clean and pluck the pheasants.

She was surprised when the men trooped heavily into the kitchen after them, the boys standing by the table rubbing their chilled hands as the father went to a cupboard and returned with a bottle of whiskey and some glasses.

He poured whiskey in the glasses, and then looked at Susan.

"Do your parents let you have whiskey?" Mr. Carlsen asked.

"They do, but I don't usually," Susan said.

"Don't feel you have to, dear," Mrs. Carlsen said. "Just because they regard it as some sort of solemn ceremony after a hunt."

"After a successful hunt," Mr. Carlsen said. "Let's drink to a successful hunt."

The boys were watching her. One by one, they picked up a glass and waited to see what she would do.

"You leave her alone, all of you," Mrs. Carlsen said, coming to her defense.

Susan picked up the glass quickly and drank it down. The men did the same thing. Susan's throat burned, and her eyes watered, and then she felt an uncomfortable warmness in her stomach.

"You're getting red in the face," Ted said helpfully.

"That I can do without," she said. She had a hard time talking. "That's horrible!"

"If she tells her father what you did," Mrs. Carlsen said to her husband, "he'll take after you with a shotgun. You ought to be ashamed of yourself."

"I don't think my father would be angry," Susan said. "I think he might laugh at me, but I don't think he'd be angry with me or Mr. Carlsen."

"Go pluck the birds," Mrs. Carlsen ordered.

Susan was surprised at the size of the lunch Mrs. Carlsen laid out, and astonished at the size of her appetite. She ate just about as much as any of the men, and with just as much relish.

Then they said their thanks and good-byes and went out to the car. On the floor on the passenger side were a dozen small packages—the cleaned pheasants.

The other two boys left as soon as they arrived at Mrs. Maroney's house. First, however, they politely shook

Susan's hand and announced they'd all have to go shooting again soon.

Then Ted took Susan into the house.

"How was it, dear?" Mrs. Maroney asked. "Are you as tired as you look?"

"Exhausted," Susan said. "But it was wonderful."

"I hate to throw you out, Deadeye," Ted said. "But I told your dad and mother I'd see you got home before dark. You'd better change."

"Is there a law that says I have to change? I think I'd rather wait until I can get in a tub of hot water."

"What about your feminine image?" he asked mockingly.

"I lost that with my first drink of straight whiskey," Susan said.

"What straight whiskey?" Mrs. Maroney asked, shocked.

"Susan took part in the sacred posthunt snort," Ted said.

"Did Mr. Carlsen know about that?"

"He gave it to her," Ted said.

"And what did Mrs. Carlsen say?"

"She was about as angry as you are, but Susan didn't fall down. She just got red in the face."

"I don't know what your mother's going to think of us, Susan," Mrs. Maroney said.

"Something nice," Susan said. "I've had a wonderful time."

"I'm glad," Mrs. Maroney said.

"Have you had your fill of hunting for a while?" Ted asked.

"I'll go tomorrow, or maybe the day after, if somebody asks me."

"How about next Saturday?" he said. "I've been asked by a friend over in your neck of the woods. I haven't seen him in a couple of years, but he said I could bring a friend with me if I wanted. His family's got some land. It will be different hunting in fallow fields rather than in cornfields. But it should be fun."

"I'd love to go."

"Set your clock for five-thirty," he said. "I'll pick you up at six."

"It's burning the back of my mouth," Mrs. Maroney said, "so I have to say it. In my day, my gentleman callers picked me up at six in the evening, not at six in the morning."

"It's kind of hard to hunt pheasant at night, Mother," Ted said.

The drive home was uneventful, but both her mother and her father were waiting for her when she got there. They seemed relieved to see her.

"We were so worried about you," her mother said.

"It was fine," she said. "There was no trouble at all."

"You do know what happened to poor Randy, don't you?" Mrs. Hebard said.

"No," Susan said. The first thing she thought was that Randy had gotten drunk again and had an accident.

"At the party," her mother said. "Those so-called nice fraternity boys stole his car and had an accident with it."

"Not when I was there," Susan said. "Ted took me home early."

"They did a pretty good job to the Wards' car, Susan," Doctor Hebard said. "Were there chaperones there?"

"I don't know," Susan said. "I suppose there were. I thought it was a very nice party."

"Aunt Marge said Randy told her that you and Ted left very early," Mrs. Hebard said. "Did you go somewhere else?"

"What are you driving at, Mother?" Susan asked.

"Let me ask the question, Susan," Doctor Hebard said. "Was there anything at the party that . . . offended you?"

"Just my beloved cousin," Susan said. "Would you mind telling me why you ask?"

"Randy's father is pretty sore," he said. "The car's pretty badly banged up."

"What's that got to do with me leaving early?"

"Randy refuses to say who he thinks stole the car," Doctor Hebard said, "and your uncle's determined to find out."

Susan was right on the verge of blowing the whistle on Randy, but at the last moment decided to hold her tongue.

"I don't really know anything about what happened to Randy," Susan said. "If anything happened, it happened after I left."

"I think you're holding something back," Mrs. Hebard said.

"How was the hunting?" Doctor Hebard asked, changing the subject.

"I got three birds with four shots," Susan said.

"Good for you," Doctor Hebard said. "Let's have a look at them."

"They're on the floor of the car," Susan said. "I'm going to go have a long hot bath."

The blisters on her feet and legs burned painfully in the soapy water, so she slumped down in the tub and rested her feet out of the water on the edge of the bathtub. And then she had a battle with her conscience.

After what Randy had done—going to Charley and making those stupid threats—she had every right in the world to tell her father what she'd learned from Ted: Randy had gotten plastered and run his father's car into the porch.

Opposed to that line of reasoning was the fact that what she knew was what the law called circumstantial evidence (or was it hearsay?). She hadn't seen Randy drunk (although, now that she thought about it, she had smelled liquor on him), and she certainly hadn't seen him run the car into the porch. If she couldn't be a witness at his trial, she had no right to squeal on him.

Moreover squealing on him would reduce her to his size.

By the time she had soaked the aches out of her muscles she had decided that she would keep her mouth shut.

13

Almost immediately she had to put her decision to the test. When Susan came downstairs after her bath, Randy and his parents were waiting for her in the living room.

Randy looked distinctly uncomfortable.

"I want to get to the bottom of this, Susan," Mr. Ward said. "Do I make myself clear?"

"The bottom of what?" Susan said. "All I know is what Daddy told me when I got home."

"But you were at the party?" Mr. Ward asked.

"Yes, I was."

"And you were aware that drinking was going on?"

"I didn't pay any particular attention to it," Susan said. "I wasn't drinking, and neither was Ted."

"But there was drinking going on, wasn't there?" Mr. Ward went on.

"You heard what she said," Doctor Hebard said.

"What would you do if your car got smashed up that way by a bunch of undisciplined hoodlums?" Mr. Ward demanded angrily.

"I don't think Susan smashed it up," Doctor Hebard said.

"But she was there."

"She was there and she left early so that she could go hunting."

"Is that why you left early, Susan?" Mr. Ward challenged. "Or was there another reason?"

"What are you suggesting?" Susan asked angrily.

"I appreciate your feeling of loyalty, Susan," Mr. Ward said. "But if there was another reason why you left early, aside from wanting to get up early, I think you have the obligation to tell me."

"If you're suggesting that I left because it was a drunken party, I'm afraid that's just not so," Susan said.

"I see," Mr. Ward said, making it perfectly clear that he didn't believe her.

"I feel very bad about this," Aunt Marge said. "If I had had any idea that this sort of thing was going on over at the university, I would certainly have said something. It's obviously not the sort of place Susan should be allowed to go."

"Just a minute, Marge," Doctor Hebard said. "Susan spent the night with an old friend of ours. From what she tells me, nothing out of place happened in her presence and I believe her. I'm sorry your car was banged up, but it has nothing whatever to do with Susan."

"You certainly have an ability to see only what you want to see, don't you?" Marge said to Doctor Hebard. She got up. "It's obvious that you're not going to get any more out of Susan than you got out of Randy," she said to her husband. "So let's stop wasting our time."

Randy had said absolutely nothing until now. Then, absolutely revolting Susan, he said: "You don't understand, Mother. You just don't go accusing your fraternity brothers of anything unless you're absolutely sure. I'll find out who did it, if you just give me a little time."

"It doesn't look as if we have much choice in the matter, does it?" Mr. Ward said. Susan saw that it was entirely possible that Randy was going to be successful in lying himself out of the whole mess.

On Wednesday she saw Alice Gunter, who smiled at her conspiratorially.

"Randy called last night," she said. "The whole thing is going to blow over. I'm glad you had enough sense to go along."

"There's a nasty word for people like Randy," Susan said. "Why didn't he just tell the truth?"

"And risk not being able to use his father's car? Don't be ridiculous."

"I thought it was pretty low blaming it on the fraternity. I'm still tempted to tell Ted how he handled it."

"You wouldn't dare do that," Alice said.

"Why wouldn't I?"

"Everybody has something they don't want generally known," Alice said. "Even you."

"What are you suggesting?"

"Oh, I just think that people might get the wrong idea about you spending all that time alone in the woods with half a dozen boys," Alice said, " 'hunting'."

"You're as rotten, as filthy rotten, as Randy," Susan said. It was the most insulting thing she could think of to say. It didn't seem to bother Alice at all.

Between then and Saturday morning Susan thought a great deal about telling Ted how Randy had lied but in the end she decided that the best thing to do was to just keep her mouth shut.

Ted showed up at five minutes to six, in what Susan decided was a disgustingly good frame of mind for that time of morning. He took over the kitchen from Mrs. Hebard, and made an unappetizing combination of ham, peppers, and onions mixed together with eggs, which he announced was a traditional hunter's breakfast.

"That makes two hunting traditions I don't like," Susan said.

"What's the other?" Ted asked, and then said, "Oh."

"What is that, a private joke?" Mrs. Hebard asked.

"Mrs. Hebard, I'm sure you will be delighted to learn that your daughter does not like straight whiskey."

"I should hope not," Mrs. Hebard said, a little uneasily, and then, apparently deciding to give Ted the benefit of the doubt, she let the subject drop.

"She has many other endearing qualities, however," Ted said. "So we'll forgive her that one weakness."

"You're in a happy frame of mind, aren't you?" Susan asked, laughing with him.

"I feel better this morning than I've felt in some time," he said.

In the car, he turned to her and said: "Would it hurt your ego terribly to know that, despite what I thought, you are not unique among the fair sex?"

"I'd be a little surprised," she said, joking with him. "I thought I was one of a kind."

"So did I until last night," Ted said, "when I broke a solemn vow to myself."

"What was the vow?"

"Never to go on a blind date, and especially never to go on a blind date when she's a relative of your buddy."

"I suppose that was the result of a painful experience?"

"It hurts me to remember how painful," he said. "But last night was an exception."

"Shouldn't I be jealous?"

"I don't think so," Ted said. "You made it pretty clear that your heart belongs to another, et cetera et cetera."

"Oh, drop dead," she said, laughing.

"As I say, I was something less than wildly enthusiastic about meeting this young lady last night. And it started like the other painful experiences, with the exception that this young lady is considerably better looking than the others were."

"And I suppose you're going to tell me all about it, detail by detail?"

"To a point. Anyway, we went through the usual busi-ness of making inane remarks to each other, punctuated by funny little smiles, and then I ran out of things to talk about like the weather, the movies, and the political situation. For lack of anything else, I announced that her relative and I were going hunting in the morning."

"And?"

"She promptly turned to her relative and asked if she could go along and if he had a gun she could borrow."

"And he did?"

"He's got almost as many guns as you do," he said.

"I gather you were out on a threesome?"

"No. There was another student nurse along. She told us that she just couldn't bear the thought of killing a poor little pheasant. That sort of killed her for the evening."

"So your unique friend is a student nurse too? From here?"

"From Patterson. She's at the hospital. I asked her if she knows your father and my father, and she does. Her name is Frances."

"And she's going with us?"

"Right," he said. "She said she'd be waiting."

"And I apparently get the relative?"

"I thought a blind date might be just what you need," he said with a smile.

"Thanks a lot, pal," Susan said. "I'll do something nice for you sometime."

"Have faith in me, Deadeye," Ted said.

"I don't have much choice, do I?" she said. She had thought somewhat selfishly that now Ted had found a girl, she would be left out. Unless of course, she hit it off with the blind date. That didn't seem likely.

Frances was waiting in the brightly lit foyer of the Student Nurses' Residence. When she saw the old Cadillac pull up, she came out to the curb.

"Bad news," she said.

"What's that?"

"I'm on duty at noon. I have to be back by then. Does that ruin everything?"

"When you're out with Deadeye and me, you'll get your limit long before then," Ted said. "Say hello to Susan and get in."

"Hi," Susan said, and smiled. She liked the looks of this girl; it was easy to see why Ted would like her.

"I know your father," she said to Susan. "You look like him."

They rode for twenty minutes out into the country, and finally turned off onto a dirt road and drove down it for half a mile until they came to a Jeep station wagon. It looked, Susan thought, like the station wagon from Charley's junkyard. When they got closer, she saw that not only was it Charley's station wagon, but that Charley himself was sitting on the hood.

He didn't seem overjoyed to see Susan.

"Miss Hebard, Mr. Kowalski," Ted said. "Oh, I forgot. You know each other."

"You've got a peculiar sense of humor, Ted," Charley said. "I told you last night her parents don't want her to be around me."

"That's just not true," Susan said.

"It isn't?" Charley asked.

"No, it isn't," Susan said.

"I have the feeling I walked in on something," Frances said.

"You are privileged to be watching one of the world's master matchmakers at work," Ted said.

"Why don't you shut up?" Charley said, interrupting Susan as she said, "Why don't you shut up?"

Charley looked at Susan. "Are you going to be in trouble with your folks because of being with me?"

"No," she said. "Clear enough?"

He smiled. "Let's go hunting," he said.

They hunted, but didn't do as well as Ted and Susan had done the week before. When they quit at half past ten, they had only two birds between them, and Susan hadn't even had a chance to fire her gun.

But as she put her gun back into its case, Susan knew she'd had a good time just walking through the fields with Charley. That triggered the memory of what Alice Gunter had said, her rotten insinuation about being alone in the woods with half a dozen boys.

She had a terrible urge to tell Ted about Randy blaming unspecified fraternity brothers for the damage done to his father's car. She suppressed the urge with an effort.

With the boys following in Charley's old station wagon, and Susan at the wheel of Ted's Fiat, they drove to a roadside diner on the outskirts of town for something to eat.

Most of the conversation in the Fiat consisted of Frances' rather flattering opinions of Ted. Frances was obviously quite taken with him, and Susan found this somehow very pleasing.

They ate a great deal, and then Ted looked at his watch.

"I've got to run Florence Nightingale back to the hospital," he said. "Do you want to take Susan home?"

"I think it would be better if you did," Charley said. "I don't want her parents to get the idea she sneaked out to meet me."

"Then wait here for me," Ted said. "I'll be back in fifteen minutes."

Predictably, during that fifteen minutes, Randy Ward walked in the diner with Alice at his side.

"Well, well," Alice said. "Look what we have here."

"Go crawl back in your hole," Susan said.

"Who is this guy?" Charley asked.

"You don't know him?" Susan asked.

"I've seen him around," Charley said. "But I don't know who he is."

"If he doesn't know you, Randy," Susan challenged, "then what was that story you told Ted?" She immediately had second thoughts, and wished that she had had the common sense to keep her mouth shut.

"What story?" Charley asked. "What's this all about?"

"Forget it," Susan said.

Randy looked trapped.

"I warned you, buddy," he said, "about staying away from Susan."

Charley looked confused, but there was still a tone of tolerance in his voice as he replied: "I don't know what you're selling, buddy. But I'd be obliged if you'd sell it someplace else."

"You know very well what he means," Alice said.

"Come on, Susan," Charley said. "I'll take you home. Ted'll know where we went when he gets here."

"Take her home, ha! Don't make me laugh," Randy said.

"Randy, why don't you shut up while you're still ahead?" Susan said.

Randy looked uncertain for a moment, and at that same moment Ted came back to the diner. The decision was made for him.

"Let's go outside, you," Randy challenged. "And I'll settle your hash."

"Just a minute," Ted said, in a very unpleasant voice, "I want to see you, Ward. I got a very interesting version over the telephone from my father of what happened at the dance. I want to know precisely what you told your father about who got drunk, and who banged up your father's car."

"I'll explain that," Randy said, uncomfortably, coloring, "just as soon as I've taught this bum that I mean what I say."

"Ted, so help me, I never exchanged two words with this nut before today," Charley said helplessly.

Randy had absolutely no alternative left but to shut Charley up at any cost. As Ted stood up, Randy threw a punch at Charley. Charley blocked it with his left arm and jabbed with his right.

It was over as quickly as it had begun. Randy fell backward onto the tile floor of the diner, and his head hit the floor with an unpleasant thump. Blood appeared at his mouth, and when he sat up, he spit a couple of teeth into his hand.

Alice Gunter started to cry. The short-order cook came on the run.

"That was smart, Charley," Ted said disgustedly, bending over Randy. The blood was now running off Randy's chin onto his shirt.

"I'm sorry," Charley said, and he looked at Susan with a helpless look of shame and frustration in his eyes. Then he started for the door.

"You stay here," Ted said. He hooked his hands under Randy's armpits and pulled him to his feet. "Did you have to hit him so hard?"

"I didn't mean to," Charley said, but he obeyed Ted's order. He didn't leave.

"He needs a doctor," Ted said. "I'll take care of him. Though I really don't know why I should. You stay here," he repeated.

"What for?" Charley asked.

"So you don't do anything else stupid until I get back," Ted said, and he led Randy, who was holding his hand to his mouth, out the door.

Alice ran after them, but stopped at the door, and shouted. "I'm going to call the cops. People like you belong in jail."

"I seen it, kid," the short-order cook said to Charley. "He swung first. But, Jeez, did you have to hit him so hard?"

"I didn't mean to," Charley repeated. He looked at Susan. "Well, I really blew it this time, didn't I? And I don't even know who he is."

"Sit down," Susan said. "And I'll explain it to you."

"I'll bring you a cup of coffee," the cook volunteered. "I don't think that broad was kidding about calling the cops. I think it would be better if it didn't look like you were running, you know?"

Charley sagged into the seat of the booth. Without quite realizing what she was doing, Susan reached over and took his hand. He looked up at her and smiled.

"I'm not too bright," he said. "You want to tell me what that was all about?"

They were still holding hands, their coffee cold and untouched in front of them half an hour later when the diner door opened and Doctor Hebard, in hospital greens, came in followed by Aunt Marge.

"Hello, Charley," Doctor Hebard said. "How's your hand?"

"All right, I suppose," Charley said.

"Let's have a look at it," Doctor Hebard said, professionally. Charley took it off his lap and laid it on the table. For the first time, Susan saw that it was wrapped in a bloody handkerchief. And she remembered then that she was still hanging tightly onto his other hand.

Doctor Hebard unwrapped the handkerchief.

"Your tetanus shot up to date?" he asked.

"Yes, sir," Charley said.

"Well, we'll go by the office and wash this out carefully," Doctor Hebard said. "Just to be sure. A skin wound made by human teeth is among the most infectious of wounds, did you know that?"

"I'm sorry I hit him," Charley said.

"And I'm sure he is," Doctor Hebard said. "You got three of his teeth, and possibly a fourth. Let's hope it teaches him a lesson."

"You don't seem very . . . upset . . . by all this," Susan said, finally putting into words what she had been thinking since her father and her aunt walked in the door.

"Well, for one thing, Charley hit Randy, not you," Doctor Hebard said. "And I am disturbed, just for the record. I'm sorry the whole thing happened. But I know where the blame lies."

"Are you going to press charges, Mr. Kowalski?" Aunt Marge asked.

"I beg your pardon?"

"It's against the law to take pokes at people," Doctor

Hebard said. "Even if you do lose the fight, it's still against the law. They call it assault and battery. It ranks right up there with drunken driving."

"Of course not," Charley said. "Why would I want to do that?"

"Thank you," Aunt Marge said. "And to answer the question in your eyes, Susan, yes, that came out, too."

"How?" Susan asked. She knew she had said nothing, and she knew Ted well enough to know that he was as sensitive about squealing as she was.

"Randy's father called Doctor Maroney, you know," Aunt Marge said, and when Susan nodded, she went on. "When Doctor Maroney wasn't satisfied with the answers Ted gave him, he called Mrs. Maroney. She went to the fraternity house and found out from the housekeeper and others what really happened last Friday night."

"I suppose I should have told you when you were at the house," Susan said to her aunt.

"Yes, you should have," Doctor Hebard said. "I understand why you didn't, but that doesn't change anything."

"I'm sorry," Susan said.

"Well, now we can start from scratch, can't we?" Doctor Hebard said. He looked at Charley. "Charley, when we finish dressing your hand, Mrs. Hebard and I would be very pleased if you'd help us eat the pheasant Deadeye here shot last week."

Charley looked at him, but didn't respond.

"It should be an interesting party," Doctor Hebard said.

"Ted will be there, of course. As a matter of fact, it was his idea. And your cousin Frances, when she gets off her shift at seven-thirty. Will you come?"

"Yes, sir," Charley said. "I'd like to."

"Marge, if you'll drop me at the hospital so I can get my clothes, Susan can drive Charley over to my office in his car," he said. "Is that all right with you, Charley? Susan driving, I mean?"

"Suits me fine," Charley said.

"I'd take you to the hospital," he said. "But if I did that, I think Alice Gunter's father would feel obligated to offer his apologies, and, unless I'm mistaken, you're just a little tired of apologies, aren't you?"

"Yes, sir. I liked what you said about starting from scratch."

"So be it," Doctor Hebard said. And then he walked out of the diner.

"You're a lot of trouble, Susan. You know that?" Charley said.

"So are you," she replied.

"I must be nuts," he said. "But I think you're worth all of it." And then, as if the speech embarrassed him, he got up quickly and walked to the door.